Love is
a time of enchantment:
in it all days are fair and all fields
green. Youth is blest by it,
old age made benign:
the eyes of love see
roses blooming in December,
and sunshine through rain. Verily
is the time of true-love
a time of enchantment — and
Oh! how eager is woman
to be bewitched!

THE CRINOLINE EMPRESS

When the beautiful Eugénie Montijo married Louis Napoleon, she became the Empress of France. But while Louis was possessed of a sensual nature, Eugénie was cold, resulting in Louis taking mistresses. Yet Eugénie maintained her dignity, winning the affection of the French people. But behind the façade of beautiful clothes and ostentatious living, she cherished a burning ambition to further the advancement of the French Empire and to ensure a secure throne for her son. Fate, however, had cruel blows to deliver.

Books by Rose Meadows
in the Ulverscroft Large Print Series:

THE CHRISTMAS REBELLION

ROSE MEADOWS

THE CRINOLINE EMPRESS

Complete and Unabridged

ULVERSCROFT
Leicester

First published in Great Britain in 1976 by
Robert Hale Limited
London

First Large Print Edition
published 1996
by arrangement with
Robert Hale Limited
London

British Library CIP Data

Meadows, Rose
    The crinoline empress.—Large print ed.—
Ulverscroft large print series: romance
1. English fiction—20th Century
I. Title
823.9′14 [F]

ISBN 0–7089–3574–5

Published by
F. A. Thorpe (Publishing) Ltd.
Anstey, Leicestershire

Set by Words & Graphics Ltd.
Anstey, Leicestershire
Printed and bound in Great Britain by
T. J. Press (Padstow) Ltd., Padstow, Cornwall

This book is printed on acid-free paper

Prologue

THE honeymoon was over. As the closed carriage turned out of the drive on to the road leading to Paris, Eugénie, seven-day Empress of France, glanced back and then with an audible sigh of relief, relaxed into the luxury of the purple velvet of the upholstery. Holy Saints forbid that she ever visited that villa again, royal residence though it might be. It would hold too many memories of distasteful, hateful incidents.

She had anticipated all the luxury and ostentation of the Palace of St. Cloud, but instead, there had been this villa with its paucity of staff and devoid of all modern amenities, simply because, Harriet Howard, the Emperor's ex-mistress had refused to vacate her suite of rooms at the palace, and the Emperor, too kind . . . or too weak . . . to insist.

"'Twill be more romantic, *ma petite*," he had whispered, as they drove out of

1

Paris . . . "just the two of us . . . alone in our love-nest . . . few prying servants . . . " Now she recalled her anger, for it was not until they were leaving the wedding reception, he had told her of the change. She smiled to herself, recalling her fit of sulks . . . her excuse to repulse his love-making.

How she detested the intimate side of marriage, so animal-like yet she had gone into it with her eyes wide open. Louis, Napoleon III of France wanted an heir to the throne . . . an heir who would be the founder of a new and glorious French dynasty . . . and she wanted power and wealth . . . she wanted to be the Empress of France.

Unseeing, she stared out of the window, her thoughts winging back over the last week. Was it possible that she might already be with child, for of course, she had had to submit. That would indeed, be the most satisfactory outcome, for once *enceinte*, there would be no further need for so called love-making . . . no need for another child. Supposing it was a girl? Would Louis insist on more children until he had a son? Bah! A woman could rule a country as well as a man. You only had to look across the Channel, where the young Victoria ruled supreme.

Slowly she turned to regard her husband, head sunk back, eyes closed. Was he asleep or just feigning? There had been a flare-up between them as they had breakfasted in her room that very morning.

"About your mother, *ma petite*," he had begun hesitantly.

"About my mother? Yes?"

"It is my wish she leaves France as soon as possible and returns to Spain . . ."

The knife with which she was buttering a roll, went down with a violent clatter.

"And why? Pray give me one good reason why she should not remain in Paris. She is growing old. She will be lonely."

With every word she uttered, she raised her voice. Poor Louis, she thought, remembering his look of alarm as he interrupted, "Eugénie . . . Eugénie . . . please. I will settle an ample allowance on her. She will not be lonely. She has your sister, The Duchess of Alba

3

in Madrid . . . her grandchildren . . . "

"I still do not see why she cannot remain here."

He had sighed and then in that quiet, firm voice she had come to know, "Because, *ma chérie*, she has always had too much influence over you. Can you not see, Eugénie, you are now the Empress of France, standing by my side. I need your womanly influence, but yours alone, not that suggested by your mother."

Of course, Louis was right and actually, she would be glad to see the back of Donna Manuela Montijo. There had never been any deep love between mother and daughter . . . a gulf that was widened, when through her mother's machinations, the young Duke of Alba had married her sister Paca, knowing full well, that she, Eugénie was passionately in love with the youth. Even now, as she thought of him, she felt the stirring of all the heartache she had suffered: still suffered, for she had never ceased to love him. Yet it was amazing, there had been no rift between the sisters, both remaining devoted to the other. Yes, it would give her great satisfaction to inform her mother of Louis' ultimatum but it would not do to let Louis know. Let him think he had wounded her.

She was not in love with him . . . had never pretended so, but she had been flattered by his violent protestations of love. She had had to play a long, waiting, skilful game, for at first, he had had the audacity to suggest she should be his mistress. With a haughty refusal, she had returned to Spain, only to find on her next visit, his ardour and desire had grown to such an extent, he was prepared to defy his ministers and the aristocracy, who regarded her as a scheming adventuress, by asking her hand in marriage.

That had been her moment of triumph, manifesting to her mother, that despite her favouritism, she had made a better match than Paca, putting those haughty aristocrats, headed by Louis' cousin, Mathilde, into their place; becoming the first lady of France; the chatelain of the Élysee, the Tuileries, St. Cloud, Fontainbleu, with Louis promising her money unlimited to decorate and furnish the palaces as she wished.

5

He had indeed, already proved his generosity in the matter of her trousseau and jewels. She had always found him tolerant and kindly . . . even mild-mannered but within these last few days she had found that behind it, there lurked an inflexible, stubborn determination. She had made this discovery, when they began to discuss household appointments.

"I have decided I shall ask M. Mérimée to be my secretary . . . "

"Never, Madame, never!"

She looked up from her writing, surprise in her query.

"And why not, sir?"

"Simply, that I do not wish our private affairs to be discussed up and down the country. He has the reputation of being the biggest gossip in France."

"You forget, sir, you insult my dead father's dearest friend . . . "

"And now your mother's dearest friend . . . "

She had screamed with rage. "How dare you, sir? What are you implying?"

"Just what all Paris has been saying for many a year. That he is your mother's lover."

She had increased the volume of her screaming; a trick she had learned in childhood. If she wanted to have her own way, just scream loud enough to intimidate her opponent; but Louis had remained almost unmoved. He had certainly appeared alarmed, looking around to see that all doors and windows were closed, until with a shrug of his shoulders, he had left the room, making no attempt to placate her. For a while, she continued to yell, hoping he would come running back but when he failed to do so she stopped with sudden abruptness. How dare he! How dare he! It was the first time she could remember her screaming to have been ineffective. Next time, she must scream louder. No man was going to master her.

Of course, she was well aware of his partiality for the opposite sex . . . a failing to which he confessed, but assuring her, that now married, he would be the most faithful of husbands. Why did women find him so desirable . . . apart from his imperial rank? He was not handsome in either face or figure. His head was too large for his short stature . . . his forehead too broad . . . his nose too prominent . . . his eyes too small, expressionless, save when a woman hove in sight. He wore his hair too long . . . his moustache too stiffly waxed to needle-point sharpness. Still, he had a certain charm. Perhaps it was his overall air of dignity, ease and courtliness.

As though aware of his wife's scrutiny, Louis opened his eyes, giving her a tender, loving smile. Caught off guard, she returned the smile, and thus encouraged, he sought her hand under the fur rug, giving it a gentle squeeze. Petulantly, she quickly withdrew it. Heavens! Given much more encouragement, he would be making love to her, here in the carriage.

Louis sighed, pulling the rug closer around him. He hated the cold, just as he disliked cold women . . . and his bride was cold . . . almost to frigidity. He had been warned. He had known of her refusal to consider all previous marriage offers; knew that she had been dubbed the Spanish Prude, but he had fallen for her radiant beauty . . . her red-gold curls twisted to hang over those glorious

8

milk-white shoulders, her pale blue eyes penetrating through all his defences. With mounting desire, he knew, that only through marriage, would she ever be his and where else would he find a woman so suited to be his Empress, with her dignified erect bearing, her classic, faultless beauty?

If only his cousin Mathilde had waited for him! But you could not expect a beautiful Bonaparte princess to wait for a man sentenced to perpetual imprisonment. Still, she should have known, that as a Bonaparte, he would find a way of escape, as indeed, he had, but too late. By the time he had escaped from the French fortress of Ham and had found sanctuary in England, she had married the wealthy Russian Baron Demidorff. Poor Mathilde, how she must have suffered, for the man was a brute and there was an early separation, Mathilde emerging as a rich young woman with a bountiful alimony.

Eugénie too, was thinking of Mathilde. Detestable creature, making it known all over Paris that Louis had pleaded with her to seek the Pope's consent for divorce so as to enable her to marry him. But Mathilde was too crafty. She was already first lady of France; hostess for Louis on every state occasion, her salon the most famous in Paris and she herself making no secret of her love for the handsome Emilien Nieuwerkerque. Now, she, Eugénie, Empress of France would show her who was the first lady, and as for her brother, that ridiculous, monocled Prince Napoleon Plon-Plon, who boasted of being the next Emperor of France, well, the sooner she gave birth to a child, the sooner he could forget it.

They had now reached the outskirts of Paris, the royal equipage commanding a certain amount of attraction but as the carriage was closed, the good folk could see little of their Majesties save an occasional white-gloved hand or a black shiny topper raised in acknowledgement and even in Paris itself, the cold, raw February fog ruled out any enthusiastic homecoming. Not that Eugénie was disappointed. She was thinking of the state ball that had been arranged for that night, two thousand guests drawn from the highest in the land, from those self same aristocrats who had scorned her as a *parvenue*. Tonight the men would perform deep respectful bows while their ladies would slowly sink down before her.

Mais oui, 1853 certainly would mark the turning point of her life.

1

FROM the railway station up to the Castle, the streets of Windsor were a colourful display of red, white and blue bunting and banners; Union Jacks fluttering side by side with the French Tricolour, for today, The Emperor and Empress of France were coming on a visit to Her Majesty.

Wonders never ceased. Why, only a few years ago, the fellow was living here as an exile, ignored by the Royal Family and everyone else at Court . . . and it was a well-known fact he was actually being kept by some wealthy woman who had fallen for his charm. Where was she now, that he had married this Spanish woman? What were they supposed to do when Their Imperial Majesties arrived? Cheer and throw their hats up in the air? Only two years ago, there had been rumours that this second Napoleon was planning to invade England. A curse on all foreigners and that included the

Queen's husband, Prince Albert. German or French, they were not wanted here. For the past two weeks, Windsor had been over-run with Froggies; servants sent in advance with wagon loads of luggage . . . grooms and stablemen in charge of fourteen horses sent over by the Emperor. Granted, they were magnificent beasts but surely the Windsor stables could have supplied all his wants. A bombastic show-off. Then there were the stories going about of the extensive redecoration being done up at the Castle. Good English money being spent on foreigners! Bah!

That morning, the townfolk had had the unexpected occasion of seeing the Queen and her brood drive through the streets to inspect and admire the decorations. But did they really need all those tutors, governesses and nurses to look after eight children?

But now, they were waiting for the visitors; curiosity over-riding their mild hostility; waiting with growing impatience for they were long overdue. What could have happened? Their ship foundered in the Channel? A train crash? Morbid speculation and rumours began to circulate along the crowded streets.

★ ★ ★

Up at the Castle, Victoria was becoming equally apprehensive. Her guests had been expected at six o'clock and strictly on time, she had come down to the Grand Hall to receive them. Now it was almost seven. Little wonder Bertie and Vicky were becoming restive. They had been meticulously instructed as to their mode of conduct and procedure but she could well remember how tedious had been her own upbringing that she could now sympathise with the children.

It wasn't only the annoyance of being kept waiting, Victoria fumed, but the delay was wearing down the confidence she had so painstakingly built up. Meeting strangers had always been a trial to her and the imminence of meeting Louis Napoleon and Eugénie was fast becoming something to be dreaded. What kind of a man was this nephew of the hated, feared Napoleon Bonaparte? A rake . . . with the reputation of being a seducer. And the Empress? An adventuress, at first they had deemed her but now grudgingly acknowledging her to be the most elegantly dressed woman in Europe. She glanced down at the blue dress she had finally chosen for this auspicious occasion, now suddenly deciding it did not become her, but too late to change.

The sudden boom of a distant gun brought everyone to their feet, quickly followed by an excited shout from the Prince of Wales, "They're coming! The train's arrived!"

A warning glance from his mother silenced him as she hastily tidied Vicky's long hair while the Duke of Cambridge attended to Bertie's bow-tie, and the correct adjusting of his jacket.

Slowly and silently the royal party moved towards the main entrance. In the distance, they could hear the unmistakeable rhythmic beat of horses' hooves, growing louder and louder. With bated breath, they listened expectantly. Nearer. Nearer. Then the Quadrangle was a babble of noise as the royal carriage and its escort of Life-Guards approached. A blare of trumpets sounded to be followed by the strains of the French national anthem, *Partant Pour La Syrie*, mingling with the clip-clop of horses and the slowing-down of carriage wheels.

As Victoria and her family stepped out on to the terrace, so the first carriage halted; the steps were down and there was Louis Napoleon kissing her hand and she, with all fears and forboding gone, actually kissing him on both cheeks! When she took Eugénie in her arms, she felt a wave of compassion and sympathy, for the Empress was actually trembling! Quickly, she brought forward Bertie and Vicky, presenting them in an easy friendly manner . . . a few moments of polite talk and then on the arm of Louis, followed by Eugénie and Albert, they were walking up the Grand Staircase, flanked by Yeomen of the Guard and so into the Throne Room. There, five more of the royal children were waiting to be presented. Louis was quick to express his delight at meeting them, while Eugénie, still somewhat restrained found conversation with Princess Victoria much easier, Her Highness being lost in admiration for her mother's elegant guest.

These pleasantries, however had to be cut short, owing to the lateness of their arrival and the little time left before dinner, Victoria herself leading them to the suite, newly decorated in their honour. Then with reassuring smiles and hopes for their comfort, she hurried away.

★ ★ ★

With the departure of the Queen, Eugénie wandered from room to room full of admiration for the decor and upholstery; the rich velvet curtains in royal purple and gold; the thick cream aubusson carpet with its bunches of pink roses; and the deep inviting chairs and sofas. It was the bed in her room, however, that fascinated her most of all with its green head, embroidered with a mocking golden eagle, topped by a canopy of feathers and all enclosed by purple satin curtains. As she continued to gaze, she could feel Louis' eyes upon her and turning and meeting them, she was quick to recognise the implication. It would never do to bar him from her bed while here as Queen Victoria's guest. A flicker of a mouè crossed her face only to disappear as she caught sight of the gold toilet-set on the dressing-table.

"The Queen's own toilet-set! How magnificent! How kind! And the flowers! Flowers everywhere!" She buried her face in a vase of enormous chrysanthemums, revelling in their tangy perfume, then looking up, said tersely, "And now, sir, I would like a few moments' rest before dressing."

Louis squeezed her hand affectionately. "I too, will be glad to get out of these trappings. You were marvellous, *ma mignonne*. I am so proud of you. I could see the Queen was most impressed . . . "

"With me? Or you?"

"You are a torment, but tonight will see the beginning of a new friendship, a strong friendship between England and France, and you, *ma perle* will be the shining light, the most beautiful, best dressed woman, the envy of all other women and the admiration of all the men . . . "

★ ★ ★

Hardly had the Emperor retired to his dressing-room, than a lady-in-waiting sought permission to speak. "Madame, the royal baggage-wagon has not arrived . . . "

Eugénie, stared at her in amazed stupefaction.

"But how . . . how can it have been delayed?"

"We cannot understand, Madame. We have made countless enquiries. Our boxes and trunks are here, 'tis but your trunks . . . all together in their special wagon . . . "

"And does that mean . . . that I have no gown . . . ?" Her voice began to rise but the unfortunate lady could think of no soothing answer.

"Don't stand there. Do something. My trunks must have arrived. Go make more enquiries . . . " and dashing over to the connecting-door, burst into Louis' dressing-room, almost screaming, "My gowns . . . my gowns have not arrived. What am I to do?"

Louis rose quickly from the bed on which he had been resting, putting an arm around her shoulder, at the same time closing the door. "Steady, chérie, steady. You must keep calm."

"'Tis easy to say that. My gowns . . . my crinolines, all specially made for this visit . . . lost . . . lost . . . "

"They will arrive tomorrow," he soothed.

"Tomorrow! But what about tonight?"

Louis was silent for a moment, then "You could plead a headache . . . "

"And stay up here alone . . . while you dine . . . and dance . . . and dally with the English ladies? Oh, no." A look of sudden determination crossed her face and breaking from him, dashed back into her room, banging the door between.

"Any news?" she demanded of the subdued ladies standing around.

"No, Madame, no . . . except . . . except that Mons. Felix is also missing . . . "

"Sacre bleu! How can he be missing? He was on the *Pelican*."

"So were your trunks, Madame . . . "

She made a gesture of resignation, at the same time giving each of her ladies a critical gaze.

"You . . . and you . . . and you . . . are of similar build to me. You say your gowns have arrived. Then I could wear one of them. Let me see your newest . . . those you have had made for this visit . . . "

With mixed feelings, the ladies displayed their latest creations, Eugénie then insisting they should model them for her further inspection. She deliberately took her time in making a decision, for inwardly she was seething with rage but only too well aware she must not make a scene . . . and she needed time to soothe her outraged sense of dignity. That this should have happened to her, the Empress Eugénie!

Her choice finally fell on a gown of smoke-grey chiffon and satin, trimmed with black lace and pink ribbon, although regrettably it had far fewer flounces than her crinolines always boasted.

After some adjustment to the waist, for she was determined not to concede one inch of her elegance, she stood back and surveyed herself in the tall pier-glass, her eyes gleaming with satisfaction, before turning and demanding, quite good-humouredly, "No sign of Mons.

Felix? Then we must manage without him."

With the assistance of her ladies, the chestnut curls were finally arranged. "I suppose 'tis the best we can manage." She frowned petulantly at her reflection. "I have a mind to dismiss M. Felix."

About to pick up her fan, she paused, moving over to a vase of chrysanthemums. Slowly, she selected several of the blooms and then, to the surprise of her ladies, carefully fixed them in her hair. With a satisfied smile, she tapped on the connecting-door.

Whatever Louis felt, he made no comment as they slowly walked down to the reception-room. Experience had taught him it was far wiser to leave the Empress to make her own decisions without any persuasions.

Eugénie, however, was feeling so self-satisfied, she could not refrain from demanding, "Well?"

"*Magnifique, ma perle . . .* "

"'Tis borrowed from one of my ladies . . . "

"Then I compliment her on her dress sense. You cannot return it, so I shall have the pleasure of providing her with another . . . "

They were interrupted by the entrance of the Queen and Prince Albert, followed by their ladies and gentlemen. As Louis kissed Her Majesty's hand, it was only with difficulty he restrained a smile for on every finger of her podgy little hands, was a heavy-jewelled ring. Even her thumbs were similarly adorned. In contrast to her stiff, over-embellished yellow gown, she wore a magnificent necklace of rubies; the whole ensemble presenting an odd picture beside Eugénie's elegance. Yet her eyes lit up with admiration as she greeted the Empress with outstretched hands, "How beautiful! How truly beautiful."

Watching the two women embrace, Louis' amusement turned to admiration, for Victoria showed no sign of jealousy . . . only genuine admiration.

★ ★ ★

Victoria was experiencing a strange elation . . . an elation never before felt . . . well, not since she was very young, when she delighted in listening to dear

24

Lord Melbourne's naughty whisperings.

She had at first, felt an odd prickly fear of Louis. He had such a bad reputation where women were concerned but then, deep down, she had always had a secret liking for these dangerous men. How often Mama had scorned her bad, Hanoverian blood.

Albert was so good . . . so considerate, a wonderful husband. He would never flirt with another woman, as Louis was now doing. Yes, that was it. This strange man, with the rapier-like moustache was flirting with her . . . the Queen of England . . . and she was enjoying it! His voice, full of charm was low and seductive; his hooded eyes, gently compelling . . . compelling her not to repulse his unspoken advances. When he took her hand and kissed it, as he did frequently, then brushed his lips against her arm, she smiled back her pleasure, oblivious of watching eyes.

She glanced across at Albert and Eugénie. Albert was actually smiling and talking animatedly with the Empress.

She turned back to Louis. He was telling her of the time when he was a

Special Constable in the Metropolitan Police.

"You one of my policemen? Why?"

He shrugged his shoulders. "To help guard Your Majesty. In those disturbed times, there was always danger of assassination. Besides, I needed occupation while waiting . . . "

" . . . To take the throne of France?"

He ignored her amused sarcasm. "Alas, I was never able to be of direct service to you. Indeed, to get near you, I found the only way was to buy a ticket for the theatre when I knew you were to be there . . . and it cost me forty pounds," he finished ruefully, only to quickly add, "But it was worth it. Throughout the whole performance, it was you I watched . . . not the stage."

"How boring," she teased.

"Boring? Never. But now, sitting here as your guest . . . it is an ambition realised." He bent and raised her hand to his lips.

It was the same pattern all the evening. When they danced, he held her closer than anyone else had ever dared, thrilling to the pressure of his hand on her plump waist, becoming more and more bemused, as he continued to murmur charming compliments.

It was in the early hours of the morning before they retired to their suites, Victoria, excited and full of animation.

"The Emperor is so very different from what I expected . . . gentle . . . full of humour . . . "

"He is a very dangerous man. Nothing will alter my opinion." There was grim deliberation in Albert's gutteral voice.

"Nonsense." Victoria's tone was placating. "And the Empress? Is she not beautiful? You liked her, did you not?"

"I found her very intelligent . . . yes . . . and beautiful."

She regarded him quizzically. She had never before heard him praise a woman. Indeed, he had paid her but few compliments throughout their fifteen years of marriage . . . and their courtship had been a very prosaic affair.

Long after he was asleep, snoring noisily, she was still awake, her excited brain recalling the sweet nonsense, Louis had been pouring into her willing ears.

Why, oh why, didn't Albert speak the same language? Of course, she loved him, as she knew he loved her, but just every now and again, it would be so wonderful to hear him say so.

2

THE visit had come to its end; six days, first at Windsor and then in London, six days of lavish spectacle, splendid banquets and magnificent balls.

Now as Louis and Eugénie took their last farewells of the Royal Family, there was genuine sorrow on both sides. Victoria and Eugénie were weeping in each others arms; the children having been repeatedly kissed but still hoping for another embrace, were crying noisily. Only Vicky and Bertie smugly kept back their tears. Eugénie had whispered to them that they were to accompany their parents when they made a return visit to France later in the year.

At last they were in the carriage accompanied by Papa and Cousin George Cambridge who were driving down to Dover with them. Last final handwaves were exchanged, a band struck up the now familiar *Partant Pour Syrie*, almost drowned by the noise of moving wheels and the jingle of harness.

Fighting to keep back her tears, Victoria turned away, dashing indoors, followed by the children up to a first floor window from where they could see the procession moving away; in time to see Louis and Eugénie stand to wave yet once again. Then pulling a bell, she indicated the children should be taken back to the schoolroom and nursery. She wished to be alone.

How wonderful it had all been. She felt she had known Eugénie all her life; already, she loved her as a sister. And Louis. Never before, had a man so stirred her. They had both deliberately sought each other's company . . . she on the pretext of state affairs . . . and he? Seducer he might be . . . his past scandalous, but listening to his flirtatious overtures, all mistrust had fled.

Albert still persisted in his dislike. Had the visit, from the political point been justified? She herself had tackled Louis on the vexed question.

"Are you still contemplating going to the Crimea?"

For answer, he had raised her hand to his lips, a gentle smile playing around that tantalizing moustache.

"You would prefer, Madam, that I did not go?"

"As head of the state, you owe it to France to remain at home . . . and to the Empress . . . "

"To the Empress? In my absence, she would make an excellent regent . . . "

"She would also make an excellent mother. You want an heir do you not? How then galavanting away to the Crimea . . . risking your life . . . leaving a vacant throne . . . "

He nodded, still smiling. "You are right, Madam. I must give the matter serious thought."

As Albert said, the man was a veritable sphinx. You never knew what he was thinking. But now, how long would it be, before the return visit to France could be arranged? She knew Louis had been vastly impressed by the military review in Windsor Park. Even there, he had been constantly in her company, riding one of his most spirited horses beside her carriage, frequently speaking with her, while all around them jogged the guard, the pick of her finest cavalry. Could the Emperor vaunt such a spectacle?

Closing her eyes, she lay back in her chair, recalling the sight and sound ... her army generals, brilliantly uniformed, bemedalled and plumed taking the salute as thousands of troops paraded in faultless step; the shouted orders ... the trundling wheels of heavy cannon ... the blaring of bugles ... the roll of drums ... all added up to one grand exciting cacophany of military triumph.

A flicker of amusement lit her face as she conjured up the occasion when she had invested Louis as a Knight of the Garter. Having kissed him on both cheeks, she had made to slip the blue ribbon over his left shoulder, but he had mistakenly presented the right. There had been some fumbling; some quiet understanding smiles, as he had whispered, *"At last I am a gentleman."*

★ ★ ★

Having remained on deck until the English coast was no longer visible,

32

Eugénie went down to her stateroom. She was tired; exhausted, not merely physically but mentally. There had been so much to learn, to absorb about English court life and protocol. Not that she had been ill at ease in the Queen's company; indeed Victoria had been most friendly. The children too, had played their part in making the visit so enjoyable. On the first morning, she and Louis had arranged a table for them ladened with toys and gifts they had brought with them, and from that moment they sought the company of Aunt Eugénie and Uncle Louis whenever possible.

Her baggage wagon, along with Monsieur Felix, had turned up the next morning giving her the opportunity of showing the Court the most beautiful gowns the Parisian couturiers could create; multi-flounced crinolines of white or pastel-shaded tulle or net, trimmed with maribou feathers or bunches of flowers; a different gown for each evening; each one more breath-taking than the last. Victoria had been voluble in her admiration but displaying no jealousy although it was obvious some of her ladies regarded the gorgeous creations with envious eyes.

It was in the quieter moments of the day however, that she had come to know and appreciate Victoria really well and strangely enough to learn another side of Louis' character . . . his love for children. Whenever they were around, he took pleasure in talking with the older ones or playing with the toddlers . . . kissing and comforting them if the occasion demanded.

Watching him romping on the lawn with them, Victoria had remarked, "The Emperor will make a wonderful papa, will he not?"

Taken by surprise, she had slowly answered. "If I ever give him a child."

Detecting a note of despondency, the Queen had drawn her down to sit on a sofa beside her, patting her hand comfortingly, "It is early days yet. Oh, I know you have suffered several miscarriages but now that your doctors are on guard, all will be well."

As she had made no reply, the motherly voice had continued, "When husband and wife are in love, it is a natural outcome, and," she added laughingly, "You do love the Emperor, do you not?"

She had been quick to reply "Of course . . . but . . . "

"I know." Again the little plump hand squeezed hers. "The trouble is, you work too hard . . . you concern yourself too much with state affairs. Now next time you find yourself . . . " Victoria sank her voice almost to a whisper " . . . the next time forget the rest of the world. Just think of yourself and the Emperor and the baby. Don't let anyone cross you or vex you . . . and you yourself . . . don't you get vexed with anyone."

She had gone on to talk of the more intimate side of marriage, a subject obviously of great interest to her. She had listened with amusement. What would Her Majesty think of that frequently bolted bedroom door?

But since that conversation, a new trend of thought had arisen. Suppose she treated Louis' lovemaking with a warmer response . . . not just dutiful submission, was it possible that next time there would be no miscarriage?

The trouble was she and Louis were

direct opposites; he a sensualist, sex meaning so much to him; but nothing to her. It was common knowledge that he had been unfaithful to her several times, throughout their brief marriage. Her first discovery stood out in her memory with loathing and distaste.

When, with angry screams she had accused him, their marriage only six months old, he had made no attempt at denial, answering her calmly, "For the first three months, *chérie*, I was wholly faithful, despite your refusals and rejections. Consider my humiliation for I am but as other men . . . and a Bonaparte . . . "

" . . . and as other Bonapartes . . . a seducer . . . a libertine . . . "

"Precisely, *ma mignonne* . . . "

"You . . . the Emperor of France . . . any woman . . . any drab . . . Never . . . never again will you share my bed . . . "

Laughing quietly, he had left her hurling lewd epithets after him, until realizing he was out of ear-shot, she had subsided in a flood of tears, knowing he would always be the victor over her or any other woman who took his fancy.

She suddenly thrust the hideous recollections away. Now was the time to start anew. Both had enjoyed a picture of royal family life. At the same time she was grateful she was not married to a man of Albert's nature. How dull Victoria's life must be, when she was not entertaining. Albert was such a bore; so staid and narrow-minded. She was sure he would never be unfaithful to Victoria.

Louis had many qualities that she admired. He was considerate and kind towards all his people; rich and poor alike. He was dedicated to the advancement of his country and in this, he always sought her advice; ready to listen to her ideas. If only they could be blessed with a child . . . a son for preference . . . she was sure they could create a happy, harmonious life together . . . but even so, would Louis be faithful?

She greeted him with a smile as he came into her state-room. He had discarded his uniform, and was wearing a long housecoat, apparently now rested, and enjoying the relaxation.

Seating himself beside her, he took

her hand. "We shall soon be home, *ma petite*, but now that we are alone, I want to thank you for your magnificent performance on all occasions . . . so regal . . . as one born royal!" He took both her hands in his, kissing first one and then the other " . . . and you yourself . . . my Eugénie . . . so very, very beautiful . . . I am so proud of you . . . "

His arms were around her, kissing her passionately and she made no resistance.

★ ★ ★

They had been back at the Tuileries a week; a week of quiet simple enjoyment without any official duties. Of course, there had been a heavy spate of letter-writing; letters of thanks to their hostess; letters to Vicky and Bertie reassuring them of their forthcoming visit; letters to her sister Paca, telling her of the pomp and ceremony of the English court, but now today she and Louis were driving through Paris to visit and inspect the recently completed Bois de Boulogne. Not really a state occasion but there would be the escort of her beloved

Cent-Gardes and the adulation of the people which always meant so much to her.

Her dresser had just fixed the last hook of her dress when the Emperor entered. From behind, he dropped a kiss on her head, "Ravishing, *ma chérie*. Ravishing."

"Have you come but to tell me that?"

"No, *ma petite*, no. The truth is I feel somewhat languid . . . for want of exercise. I have therefore asked Edgar Ney to ride with me . . . "

"To ride? Where?" There was annoyance in her voice.

"Oh, have no fear, *ma mignonne*. I do not intend you to visit the Bois de Boulogne alone. I too, want to see the progress. No, I suggest you drive in the carriage with one of your ladies. Let the people see their beautiful Empress . . . let them give you their undivided acclamation. Ney and I will ride quietly along within a few minutes of your departure . . . "

She sighed, "I would prefer to be accompanied by you . . . "

"Nonsense, *chérie*. I have already

given the order for my horse to be saddled . . ."

"You could countermand the order . . ."

He kissed her again. "As I said, Eugénie, I feel the need of exercise," and turning on his heel, left the room.

As her bonnet, a creation of white silk, its pleated brim adorned by bunches of violets, was now carefully placed in position, she scowled at her reflection. Louis was so clever at getting his own way without really quarrelling . . . always managing to have the last word.

Once seated in the carriage, however, her high spirits quickly returned, as the Cent-Gardes, heading the procession, moved out of the gates to a great roar of welcome, their tunics blue as the April sky; their gleaming cuirasses giving off lightening-like shafts of brilliance.

Eugénie waved in response, but today in a more restrained genteel manner; the manner she had learned from Victoria. It was the same all the way along the new roads built since Louis became Emperor; roads, straight and wide to cut down the risk of sudden attack or assassination. Gone were the narrow alley-like streets and blind corners. New mansions, hotels and shops had taken the place of the former ancient decrepit buildings, built in wide squares with fountains playing in the centre; beds of flowers everywhere, fuchsias, begonias, geraniums, all flaunting their beauty. Even the street lamp standards were of such ornate design as never before seen.

As the carriage bowled along the Champs Eliseés, she glanced up at the house she had bought for Paca and her family to enable them to visit Paris whenever they wished, for Paca had no liking for court life.

A wave of nostalgia swept over her as the image of James, Duke of Alba floated before her eyes. She still loved him, not in any sensual way but as the shining knight of her childhood dreams. The Holy Virgin be praised that the bond of love between her and Paca was as strong as ever.

She roused herself to respond to still louder acclamations, as orders were shouted to the escort and the carriage came to a standstill. She had been so lost in her thoughts, so enclosed by the guard, that she had seen little of the landscape but now, as the troops reformed, she exclaimed in delight.

Stretching away in the distance was a vista of green, smooth grassland, interspersed by innumerable pathways, shadowed by myriads of trees. In the distance was the glint of ornamental lakes, more fountains and everywhere a profusion of flowers in beds, borders and in baskets hanging from ornamental poles and lamp standards; in tubs at the intersection of pathways; flowers, flowers everywhere . . . and all this beauty due to her and Louis . . . and of course to Baron Haussmann, who had transformed their dreams into reality.

There was still much to do. France was to become the leading country of Europe; Paris the centre, where everyone who was anyone would congregate; the rich and the intellectuals; artists, writers and musicians; a city of gaiety and beauty. But Louis had greater plans . . . plans to expand the French Empire, to bequeath a really worthwhile heritage to those who should come after him.

She must give France an heir, for she

was now determined, cost what it may, she and Louis should be the founders of a new and lasting dynasty. Since their return from England, they had lived on the most amicable of terms, though there had been occasions when she had wanted to scream she preferred to be alone . . . to plead fatigue or a headache . . . but she had managed to fight down the impulse.

She looked along the route. What was keeping Louis? Surely he should be here by now. He and Edgar Ney had been at the gates of the Tuileries, giving her the most royal of salutes as she passed through. Her impatience began to grow. Then the clip-clop of horses drawing nearer, the rising crescendo of cheering . . . then Louis reining in his horse beside her carriage and for the benefit of those watching, she was giving him the warmest of smiles . . . a smile that quickly froze as she recognised a look of strain not only on his face but on the faces of those accompanying him.

He bent over the carriage, his voice a whisper . . . "Keep smiling, *ma petite.* There was an incident along the route

. . . nothing to fear . . . no-one was hurt . . ."

She could not hold back the tremor in her voice, "An attempted assassination?"

He ignored the question. "We are returning now, the Empress showing no fear. Smile my Eugénie. Smile."

The escort had closed around them; the procession was moving off, the horses swinging into a faster pace than usual, Eugénie doing as Louis had bid, smiling, apparently unmoved; the people acclaiming them louder than she could ever recall.

Reaching the Tuileries, Louis was quick to dismount, giving his arm to aid Eugénie into the Palace. Hurrying into a ground floor room, she threw herself on to a sofa, bursting into violent sobs.

Louis was on his knees beside her. "There, *ma petite*, there," he consoled. "It was an act of Providence I was not in the carriage with you. Even so, no harm was done . . . "

Her weeping suddenly ceased. "Tell me what happened," she asked bleakly.

Louis shrugged his shoulders. "Very

little. We were riding along . . . slowly
. . . when this fellow stepped out of the
crowd and came towards me as though
to present a petition . . . then . . . ”
"Then?"
"Then he fired at me . . . and missed."
He laughed mirthlessly. "The police had
no difficulty in arresting the blackguard."
"Who is he?"
"A young Italian. Evidently resents our
occupation of Rome. Pianori, by name
. . . But come . . . let your ladies take
you up to your room . . . ”
For answer Eugénie burst into another
paroxysm of tears, moaning, "All to
no purpose . . . all the tranquillity
. . . the peace . . . the submission . . . all
wasted."
He looked at her in bewilderment,
wondering if the shock had been too
much for her, "Of what are you speaking,
ma mignonne?"
"I am speaking of . . . of my hopes of
ever bearing a child. How can I hope to
do so, when danger stalks us every time
we go out . . . when I can have no peace
of mind . . . ”
"You are overwrought, *ma petite,*

Doctor Conneau shall prescribe a sedative for you . . . "

Yes, there was wisdom in what Victoria had said. His first duty was to remain here in France with Eugénie . . . he would not be going to the Crimea.

3

EUGÉNIE was in a tizzy of excitement. The great day had arrived. Already, Victoria and Albert accompanied by Louis would be driving through Paris. She just couldn't wait for the moment when she and Victoria would be alone . . . alone to discuss the most wonderful subject imaginable . . . her pregnancy, now two months advanced. Of course, she had written the Queen as soon as the doctors had confirmed her condition and with equal promptness, back had come Victoria's reply, admonishing her to take the greatest care, to rest and to avoid all fatigue concerned with their impending visit.

For the last three months, the workmen of Paris, had been feverishly labouring in relays round the clock, so that more hotels, mansions and tree-lined boulevards should be completed in time for this visit. More parks had been landscaped, more ornamental lakes and fountains sending their spray high into the air.

Yesterday, after Louis' departure for Boulogne, she had slipped out of the Palace by a side-gate, and in a carriage devoid of any coat of arms, and accompanied by only a lady-in-waiting, she had driven through the city joining the long un-ending stream of vehicles, just two more ladies admiring the decorations, their faces hidden beneath dainty parasols.

From every building, flags, banners and bunting fluttered joyously, a riot of red, white and blue; union jacks alongside the tri-colour. Flowers of every hue somehow entwined with blossom and foliage around lamp-standards and pillars, joining to form festoons over the roadways. Every doorway boasted its hanging-basket; every niche a tub. Paris was a profusion of flowers, and today, to add to the lavishness of colour, 60,000 troops were lining the royal route.

Mathilde had declared it too vulgar; too ostentatious; indeed she deplored the atmosphere that was gradually taking hold of the city but then, Mathilde preferred the intellectuals at her salon, while she and Louis preferred beautiful women and handsome men around them; the laughter and gaiety of the theatre. She smiled inwardly as she recalled one of Victoria's requests, concerning their entertainment. Would dear Eugénie be careful about choosing the theatres they would be visiting . . . on account of the children, of course. She had heard that some Paris theatres were rather licentious. Her amusement continued as she recalled some of the shows she and Louis had recently seen . . . actresses almost naked . . . songs bawdy and lewd but the music so infectious.

The muffled boom of cannon roused her. The procession was nearing St. Cloud. With a last glance in the mirror she went out to join Mathilde waiting at the top of the Grand Staircase. Now through the open windows they could hear the military bands; the roar of the cheering crowd and then the clatter of horses' hooves and finally the stillness as revolving wheels came to a halt.

With an almost suffocating sense of

49

pride she glanced down the serried row of Cent-Gardes lining the staircase. Surely Victoria would be aware that they were the equal if not superior to her Life-Guards; everyone over six foot in height, all trained to the ultimate perfection in military discipline and bearing. She could never forget the occasion, when, on their first spell of official duty, lining the staircase at the Tuileries, she had been so tantalised by their statuesque immobility, that she had struck one across the face to test his reaction. The man had not moved a muscle nor flickered an eyelid, but Louis had been furious, taking her to task at the first opportunity.

"Why . . . why did you so degrade yourself?"

"'Twas but a matter of amusement. I wished to discover . . ."

"What you discovered, Madam, was that the man possessed more dignity than the Empress of France," he had stormed.

She had been mortified, especially as Mathilde had witnessed the incident. She would never commit such a *faux pas*.

Now Mathilde was waiting to be

presented to the Queen of England, who at this moment was walking up the staircase on Louis' arm, followed by Mathilde's brother, Plon-Plon and Prince Albert. Behind them came the Prince of Wales and his sister, the Princess Royal. There were the official greetings; the official presentations, but over all, there were the warm smiles of friends re-united, two happy children trying to hide their excitement.

Eugénie lost no time in taking her guests to the suite she had had prepared for them, every room re-decorated in white and gold. Responding to their exclamations of delight at the spacious rooms and the beautiful views from the windows, she volunteered, "These were the apartments occupied by her Late Majesty, Queen Marie Antoinette."

Bertie's eyes widened with interest. "Does her ghost ever walk?" while Vicky momentarily saddened, could only murmur, "The poor, poor dear queen."

Now began ten days of state drives and visits during the day, to be followed by a ball, banquet or a theatre in the evening. Acting on the doctor's orders and Victoria's insistence, Eugénie missed the daytime functions, only appearing in the evenings looking more radiant than ever.

At the very first opportunity, Victoria had opened the subject uppermost in her mind, "My dear, there is one service, which I insist you will allow me."

"And that is, dear sister?"

"I will choose the nurse for your baby. An English nurse. English nannies are so reliable. No nonsense about them."

Eugénie hesitated. "As yet, I have not given any thought . . . "

"Nor is there any need for you to do so. Leave the matter with me. Another thing, dear Eugénie, forget all fear of pain. There is now such relief for childbirth pains. Chloroform . . . "

"I have heard of it, but . . . "

"I can recommend it. My doctor administered it at the birth of my last child. Just a pad over your nose, then oblivion until they put the babe in your arms."

"I do not think the French doctors are in favour . . . "

"Why not?"

"It is contrary to the teaching of the church."

"Then I shall speak to the Emperor. I am sure he will not wish his Empress to suffer."

She smiled as she recalled some other snippets of their conversation. Victoria was by no means inhibited when it came to passing on, or listening to a spicy tit-bit of gossip. She had confessed to a curious liking to sit with any of her friends or ladies-in-waiting when they were in child-labour. She prided herself that her company was of great benefit just as she was sure her advice in April had brought about Eugénie's present condition. Well, she had certainly taken her advice to heart.

It was most gratifying that Victoria had been impressed by the Cent-Gardes, so much that she spent a considerable amount of her leisure time sketching them and the colourful Zouaves. It was during these quiet periods that the Prince of Wales sought out Louis, asking questions about French history. They were to be seen walking about the gardens in a most companionable way, the Emperor's arm around the boy's shoulder. At the same time, the Princess Royal was, at her invitation, enjoying a private display of the Imperial ball-gowns and crinolines, going into raptures as gown after gown was brought out for her inspection.

"There is no-one in London who can create such ensembles," she sighed. "When I am older and have my own allowance, I shall come to Paris for all my clothes . . . "

"And I shall take you to my dressmakers and help you choose . . . "

"Will you help choose my wedding-gown?"

"Your wedding-gown?"

"Oh yes. Mama is already advising me."

Eugénie looked troubled. Victoria had confided she was in favour of a marriage between her daughter and Prince Frederick of Prussia . . . but Vicky was only fifteen, without any knowledge of the world . . . or men.

She was well aware Victoria was again wallowing in Louis' honeyed whisperings, for no lover could be more attentive, despite the Queen's bad taste in dress and the amused titters of some of the French ladies.

Last night there had been the ball at the Hotel de Ville, where in the almost overpowering atmosphere of eight thousand guests and masses of heavily perfumed hot-house flowers, Victoria and Louis had danced untiringly. She had worn a gown of white silk, heavily embroidered with scarlet geraniums, but it was the display of diamonds that had set everyone talking, diamonds on every finger; at her wrists and round her throat, while on her hair, flashing from a diadem was the fabulous Koh-i-Noor.

Yet her day-time ensembles came in for much more severe criticism, Eugénie frequently overhearing snide remarks.

"She has no sense of style or colour . . . "

"That hideous green parasol . . . "

"Those bonnets! So massive! So old-fashioned!"

"Those huge feathers! So outmoded!"

"And her shoes! Low-heeled and tied with ribbon . . . "

"And her reticules! All home-made . . . "

"Have you seen the one embroidered with the multicoloured parrot?"

"That is her favourite. I heard her tell the Empress one of her daughters had embroidered it . . . "

It wasn't only the French ladies who criticised; many of the Queen's household joined them, deploring their mistress's lack of dress sense.

"If only she could be influenced by the Empress, then we too, could wear more modish styles."

For the second half of their visit, the Court had moved to the Tuileries and for their farewell assembly, there had been a ball at Versailles, where, under the glare of the huge chandeliers, Louis and Victoria had danced, while Eugénie had watched without any rancour that she was denied the gaiety. Her daily, intimate conversations with the Queen had cemented their friendship still closer and despite Albert still remaining somewhat remote, the alliance between France and England was stronger than ever.

★ ★ ★

Waiting on the terrace for the Queen and Prince Albert, Eugénie and Vicky watched the Emperor and Bertie strolling towards them, talking in their usual confidential manner. As they came to a halt a few steps away, Eugénie could not restrain a smile as Bertie remarked, *"You have a nice country, sir, I wish I was your son."*

"Sh . . . Sh . . . " came Louis' whisper, "You must not let your papa hear that."

For answer, Bertie moved nearer Eugénie. "Aunt Eugénie, could not Vicky and I stay a few days longer? Please?"

For a moment, she was nonplussed. Then gently, "But your Mama and Papa could not spare you."

"Could not spare us? There are six more at home and they don't want us."

By now their parents had joined them, putting an end to Bertie's plea and the ladies were in each other's arms weeping more copiously than they had done at their last parting; but Victoria managing to give a few last words of advice and Eugénie begging that she and the Prince would again visit them in the near future. In the meantime, with a fatherly hand on Bertie's shoulder and an arm around Vicky, Louis was propelling them towards the carriages, tears streaming down Vicky's face, despite Uncle Louis was travelling with them as far as Boulogne. A last embrace . . . a last kiss and Eugénie was standing alone; the band playing first the English national anthem . . . then 'Partant Pour Syrie'. Then one last handwave.

4

LOUIS was bored . . . frustrated, in an all-round state of ennui. Christmas had come and gone with its usual festivities but whether at Compiègne, St. Cloud or the Tuileries, he could find no enthusiasm for the hunt or fancy dress ball or any other diversion arranged by the Court. Perhaps it was because Eugénie took no part, save sit around, watching . . . watching him . . . in her pregnancy more beautiful than ever . . . more remote . . . more unattainable.

As his carriage bowled along towards la rue de Courcelles, the home of his cousin Princess Mathilde, he pondered on the possibility of finding some relief for his tedium. It wouldn't be in her salon, where high-brow musicians and world-famed singers would be performing but there was always the possibility that some roguish little lady-in-waiting or guest would be a willing partner to any suggestion he might make.

When Eugénie's doctors confirmed she was with child, his delight had been so overwhelming, his concern for her wellbeing so great, that he had vowed it would be no hardship to be celibate, no matter how long it might be necessary. Eugénie, however had shown little appreciation of his good intentions. Whether it was mere feminine tantrums . . . or a more spiteful mode of punishing him for past misdemeanours, she would plead her condition at the first suggestion of any amorous overture. When he longed to take her in his arms, to thank her for the great gift she was about to give him, she would shrug him off and turn her head away from the proffered kiss. Was it to be wondered that on occasion he had fallen by the wayside? Of course it had always been with the utmost discretion. Nothing must reach Eugénie's ears . . . no involvement with the lady . . . just a mere peccadillo.

Mathilde greeted him with warmth, her softness and perfume sending his thoughts winging back to when he had first held her in his arms . . . a boy and a girl . . . first love . . . pure and wonderful.

If only she had had faith in him, she would now be the Empress of France.

She led him to a chair beside her own, asking with exaggerated concern, "Empress? I expected her to accompany you?"

"She sends her regrets. Unfortunately she has a migraine."

Mathilde laughed softly. " 'Tis odd. Her migraines always coincide with my invitations."

Louis shrugged his shoulders. How ill-natured women could be one against the other. It was only too true. There was no love lost between the two ladies.

From an adjoining salon, came the strains of soft, seductive music. "Shall we go through, Louis . . . ?"

He laid a restraining hand on hers. "I think not, I am in no mood. Have you no interesting people with whom I can talk?"

She pondered for a moment. "There is a couple newly come from Italy. You might find them of interest."

She called a page to her side giving him

instructions to search the salons for the Count and Comtesse de Castiglione.

Louis' eyes moved restlessly over the stream of guests passing before him. There were many inviting glances from certain ladies but he was feeling the need of real excitement. Then he was aware of Mathilde presenting the Italians. He took little notice of the man, but as the lady slowly rose from her obeisance, his first reaction was one of surprise. She was but a child . . . a young girl . . . a beautiful girl, but showing no pleasure or excitement at being presented to the Emperor of France.

Pale pink feathers stirred but gently in her black silky hair, while her simple dress of straight design, and almost transparent material displayed the beautiful contours of her young, trim body.

Mathilde had already inveigled the Count away leaving Louis to entertain the lady, but for once he felt out of his depth, just gazing at her, twisting and twirling his moustache. She was a married woman, yes, but she appeared so young . . . so naïve . . . so innocent.

He rose, taking her hand, leading

her to a sofa in a secluded corner, marvelling at her fragility and light-footed movement, almost ethereal.

"You will not have been married long?" was his opening gambit.

"Six years, sir."

"Six years!" He could not restrain the surprise in his voice.

"I was married at the age of fourteen, sir."

Her voice was leaden and dull, betraying no interest in continuing the topic.

Vainly he tried to make conversation, but the Comtesse was either being maddeningly reticent or terribly shy, forcing him to cut short their stay and return her to her husband.

As he took leave of his hostess, Mathilde, with amusement in her eyes, asked "Well?"

"She is beautiful but lacks intelligence."

Yet he could not erase her from his mind. He must see her again. He took to accepting every invitation, hoping she would be present but it was three weeks before he was successful.

He had spent a dull, unrewarding evening at a concert given by his Uncle

Jerome, and it was with a nagging feeling of frustration that he excused himself shortly before midnight. Going down the main staircase, he came to an abrupt halt as he saw the Comtesse approaching, her dress of silver lamb shimmering under the candelabras.

"You are arriving late, Madam," he said testily.

"You mean you are leaving early, sir," was the pert retort, a mischievous smile playing around her mouth. So she could smile! He needed no further invitation, turning and walking back upstairs, his arm around her slender waist.

★ ★ ★

Virginia, Comtesse de Castiglione, scowled, as her cousin, Count Cavour, Chief Minister to his Majesty, King Victor Emmanuel of Italy, came into her room.

"I heard dear Louis' carriage drive away," he began.

" . . . So you thought to come and enquire as to what progress I am making. None, sir. None. There he

64

sits, everlastingly twirling that moustache, saying little but giving me boring details as to the Empress's state of health. Indeed, I shall be as relieved as the lady when the child is born."

"Poor Virginia. But to say you are making no progress . . . no. Apart from the information you have already passed on to me, you are consolidating the groundwork for when you . . ."

" . . . For when I become his mistress? Bah! When will that be? Two months I have known him and beyond an occasional kiss or tightened clasp around my waist . . . and he supposed to be Europe's most lecherous man . . ."

"You will not have much longer to wait. Once his Empress has given him his heir . . ."

"Surely he will then be more devoted to her . . . ?"

"For a few weeks, maybe . . . but then, I have been making enquiries and have learned much."

She raised puzzled eyebrows. "The Epress is a cold frigid woman," he went on, "already openly telling her ladies, there will be no more children . . . that she intends to avoid the intimate side of marriage, so you see my dear Virginia, it will be easy for you."

"And what will be my reward?"

He laughed. "Will not the honour of being Maîtresse de Titre to the Emperor of France, be sufficient reward?"

"No, it will not. In return for supplying the Italian government with vital French information, Victor Emmanuel promised me rewards beyond my wildest dreams . . . "

" . . . and those promises will be honoured. All you have to do, is to win the Emperor's confidence, but in doing so, take advantage of all the good things that come your way and enjoy the liaison with him."

She sighed, "But the waiting time, is mighty tedious."

Count Cavour's voice took on a harsh, grim note.

"Whatever methods you use, succeed, my cousin, only succeed."

★ ★ ★

The heavy rain, whipped by the March wind was beating an irregular tattoo on the windows of the Tuileries . . . windows that were as brilliantly lit as on nights when Eugénie was holding one of her renowned assemblies. Carriages were rolling up and setting down their occupants; members of both families and important dignitaries of Church and State, for the Empress had begun her labour. There was an air of bewilderment among them, as to who were entitled to places of honour, for notice of the immediate birth had come as a surprise, the baby not being expected for several days. There was the same bewilderment down in the royal kitchens, for they too had been taken unaware; no preparations for the refreshing of this unexpected influx.

Above the confusion of footmen ushering the visitors up to Eugénie's apartments; housemaids, with cans of hot water dashing along the corridors, could be heard the imperious voice of the Comtesse de Montijo, directing the callers into adjoining rooms . . . even screaming at the doctors and midwives as to how they should proceed with her daughter's confinement.

Louis, on the doctor's suggestion, had left the bedchamber, only too glad to escape the torture of seeing Eugénie rolling in agony, unable to hold back her moaning, but now, pacing the long corridor, was suffering an even worse torture of imagining what might be the outcome.

It was when his cousins, Princess Mathilde and her brother, Plon-Plon arrived, that along with them he re-entered the bedchamber, going down on his knees, to take Eugénie's hot hand in his, murmuring loving comfort, unaware of Plon-Plon's malicious gag. Anna Manuela, however was quick to notice his expression and fearing for Eugénie, grabbed hold of him, with total lack of ceremony, pushing him behind a screen with a curt, "You sit there."

Midnight came and went, the weary visitors dozing in their chairs, dozing that was constantly interrupted by Eugénie's agonised groans. Dawn broke over the palace, without any news for the swarms of reporters, but with the serving of hot coffee, renewed hope came that soon the child must be born and they could go home, for as they listened they could hear the moans were now more frequent . . . more highly-pitched, moans that left her so short of breath, that the doctors had to walk her about the room to restore her natural breathing.

All night long, Louis had paced to and fro hoping any moment to hear the cry of his first-born, but daylight found him haggard and distraught.

Did all women suffer when giving birth? Had Alexandrine Vergeot suffered when giving birth to his two bastard sons? She had never complained. The thought was but momentary. He felt no guilt. No compunction. He had never seen her since before the birth of the second boy. He had provided for her and had attended to the boys' education. She belonged to the far-distant past. This baby, his and Eugénie's child, was the future ruler of France.

Morning became noon. More visitors had arrived from more distant places, but Louis would see none of them. Where they had laughed and joked about the 'expectant father' they now saw an almost tragic figure weighed down by grim forbodings, for it was obvious the Empress's condition was giving rise to great anxiety. Could nothing be done to help her . . . to lessen the agony? What about chloroform as advocated by Queen Victoria? The doctors did not advise it saying the anaesthetic delayed delivery.

Dusk was falling. The gas-lights were going on again within the palace. By now, vast crowds of loyal Parisiens, had gathered . . . waiting. Midnight came but few had gone home.

Louis was now experiencing a terror, he had never before known. How could Eugénie go on enduring such agony? When he again ventured to her bedside, he could read the fear on the face of the doctors. It was in the early hours of the morning they came to him, still pacing the corridor . . . He turned quickly, sobs punctuating his voice, "The child . . . the child . . . has been . . . born?"

The doctor hesitated. "Alas, sir, no . . . and now . . . it is . . . it is our fear, that we cannot save both mother and child . . ."

"Great God!" There was agony in his ejaculation, then angrily, "Well, you

70

fools, what is delaying you?"

"You must instruct us, Sire. The mother or the child?"

Louis drew in a sharp breath, then, almost shouting "How can you ask? The mother of course. My wife. The Empress."

Now the pacing began again. There was to be no heir to the throne of France for how could he expect Eugénie to undergo such suffering again? His cousin Plon-Plon would inherit the throne . . . and his children after him . . . despite the fact that the people of France detested Plon-Plon.

A sudden shrill cry burst upon his thoughts. The cry of a baby? Did that mean that Eugénie . . . ?

He dashed into the room. The doctors were bent over the bed. A midwife was holding a blanket-wrapped bundle but Louis had eyes only for the still figure on the bed. A nurse barred his way. "Not just yet, sir . . . "

"The Empress . . . ?"

"She is well, sir."

" . . . and the baby?"

"Here sir. A fine boy, sir . . . "

71

Louis looked down at the minute, red face of his son, born but a few minutes ago. Then the woman's words penetrated. "A boy? You said a boy?" Suddenly he let out a yell, rushing from the room, only pausing to kiss the midwives . . . almost causing a maid to drop her tray as she too was kissed boisterously first on one cheek and then the other.

He had a son. France had a Prince and God be thanked, Eugénie had come through her ordeal safely.

* * *

Throughout the whole of France, guns roared out a salute of welcome to the little newcomer. Paris was delirious with joy. In preparation for the birth, the citizens had already presented Eugénie with a cradle of gold, fashioned in the shape of a Norman boat, the Imperial Eagle rearing it's proud head at the helm. Now Louis was quick to respond; money for the poor; money for the advancement of the arts; an amnesty for political prisoners.

72

When the doctors informed him that it would not be safe for Eugénie to bear another child, he was not unduly dismayed, or even concerned. What did it matter? He had a son. France had an heir to the throne. Yet as soon as she began to recover her health and strength, he again quizzed the doctors in more detail as to the prospect of his marital future, being much relieved to learn that there was no impediment whatever to normal married life.

As soon as the christening had taken place it was their intention to go to their summer villa in Biarritz. There, away from all state duties he would have time to woo her again, their baby son drawing them closer than they had ever been.

Eugénie, however, considering she had performed her duty both to Louis and France, plaintively rejected him the first time he sought her bed, pleading her still weak state of health.

"But, Eugénie, *ma mignonne*, you cannot deny me any longer. I love you. I need you."

She laughed derisively. "*That is all you*

men ever think of. There are other forms of love."

"For instance?"

"Our mutual love for our son. Our love of France."

He shook his head in bewilderment. "But a man needs a woman . . . ."

"You have never had any difficulty in finding one," she scoffed.

He had left her, too shocked to retaliate. Was she so indifferent to him that she was not even jealous? During the weeks, both before and after the birth, he had been wholly faithful to her despite the knowledge that Virginia would be a most willing mistress. They still frequently met at the various salons; he studiously correct; she deliberately seductive. Remembering Eugénie's agony, how could he be otherwise?

★ ★ ★

A gentle perfumed breeze was wafting through the streets of Paris on the June evening that the now three months old Prince Imperial was christened at Notre

Dame, receiving the names, Eugénie Louis Napoleon, though to his doting parents he was always, Lou-Lou. As usual, given any occasion, Paris was wearing her gayest apparel, as only Paris knew how; the traditional flags and bunting; the profusion of flowers; the military bands; orchestras from the music halls and countless groups of amateur musicians, flocking crowded pavements; men and women, home from work wearing their Sunday best; the street-walkers in their gayest, most daring finery, more heavily made up than usual to denote their trade, knowing there would be some wealthy patrons about.

The banquet at the Hotel de Ville that followed the ceremony, embraced royalties, statesmen and Church dignitaries from every corner of Europe. It seemed as though the birth of the Prince had brought peace and understanding among them, as they discussed their problems to the music of lilting orchestras; the high-pitched chatter of the ladies and the bawdy laughter of the men.

As Louis and Eugénie chatted with their guests, everyone remarked on the beauty of the Empress; the good fortune of Louis and their obviously happy marriage. It was not until the early hours of the morning, that they were at last free to return to the Tuileries. Dawn was already breaking, but the streets were still crowded; the merry-making was still going on; the daughters of joy, reaping a rich harvest. Again, Louis could not restrain the tears, lifting Eugénie's hand to his lips, remarking, *"This christening has done us more good than our coronation."*

★ ★ ★

It had been a long, arduous continuity of evening stretch into night and then into morning, but Louis was feeling too exhilarated . . . too excited to go to bed. He was filled with a desire to take Eugénie in his arms to kiss and hold her close; to beg her to forget her inhibitions about love.

When he entered her room, she was already in bed, a small bedside candelebra illuming her face. Meeting her cool gaze, he felt his high spirits

76

spiralling downwards, giving rise to a stupid uncertainty as to how he should approach her.

For several moments he strode about the room, before going to sit on the bed and asking with an assumed note of gaiety, "How soon can we leave for Biarritz?"

"I can be ready tomorrow . . . "

He laughed, his good humour returning. "That's a little too soon for arranging of certain state matters . . . and have we not an evening fête at Villeneuv-l'Étang in about a fortnight's time?"

"Ah yes . . . but we could make preparations to leave immediately after."

"That would be splendid. Oh, Eugénie, *ma perle*, how I am longing to have you all to myself; away from state duties; away from the Court; away from critical prying eyes; away from the everlasting wagging tongues . . . "

"If there was naught for prying eyes to see there would be naught for wagging tongues to repeat."

He looked at her keenly, detecting the note of iciness in her voice. "Just what are you trying to say, Eugénie?"

"I am tired, Louis. We will talk in the morning."

"No, we will talk now."

"Very well, but 'tis a pity such a wonderful day should be marred." She sighed deeply and then angrily burst out, "I am given to understand, you are acquainted with a certain Italian lady . . . "

"You mean the Comtesse de Castiglione?"

"Is that the creature's name? I hear that you have been visiting her frequently."

"I have encountered her at various functions and have on occasion escorted her home."

"She is married, I am told."

"She is."

"And you are cuckolding the poor simpleton of a husband? Oh, Louis, how naughty of you."

"Eugénie, stop this ridiculous banter."

"Ridiculous! I say disgusting. You visit this . . . this . . . light-of-love late at night . . . come creeping back in the early hours of the morning . . . and then . . . then . . . you come seeking entry into my bed."

"If you are inferring that I have shared

that of the Comtesse, you have been basely mis-informed." His voice was agitated. "Listen, Eugénie. I swear to you, I have never been unfaithful to you since . . . "

"Since the last time," she interrupted vulgarly.

He rose, bending over her, his hands on the pillow, either side of her head. "I swear to you, Eugénie, there has never been anything of an intimate nature between me and the Comtesse. You must believe me."

She attempted to rise; to push him away. "Please, Louis. I dislike your histrionics as much as I dislike your love-making."

He straightened himself with a gesture of hopelessness. Why did he go on loving her when she so constantly rejected him?

★ ★ ★

She was busy writing to Victoria, telling her of yesterday's ceremony and the progress of her beloved baby, not forgetting to add fulsome praise concerning Miss Shaw, who Her Majesty had recommended to be her head nurse. Miss Shaw was indeed a treasure. Never would she be able to thank dear Victoria for being so kind. She put down her pen as Louis entered the room, smiling up at him as though last night had never happened. Most likely come to say he was sorry; that he would see the Italian baggage no more.

"You can take up your pen again," he said curtly, "and add to your list of guests for the evening fête the name of the Comtesse de Castiglione."

She felt the colour rush into her cheeks. "I will not! How dare you invite the woman to meet me?"

"Unless you instruct your lady-in-waiting to send the invitation, I shall invite her . . . and escort her to Villeneuve l'Étang myself . . ."

She began to shout abuse at him, raising her voice to a high screaming pitch, but Louis, merely shrugged his shoulders as he walked away, pausing only at the door, to say quietly, "Do not forget to send the invitation."

As the door closed, she pounded the desk with her fists. How dare he? How dare he so humiliate her? But she knew humiliation would be far greater if the Emperor was to bring the creature as his special guest. Thank God they would be going to Biarritz the following day.

5

SEATED on the lawn of Villeneuve
l'Étang, Louis and Eugénie greeted
their guests. Wearing a pastel
shaded crinoline in a light summery
material, Eugénie looked cool and relaxed,
but deep down, she was full of
apprehension. When that woman arrived,
how was she going to deal with her? She
glanced at Louis. He too appeared fidgety
and ill-at-ease, everlastingly turning to
look in the direction where vehicles of
every description were continually arriving.
When he let out an excited exclamation,
she could not resist following the line
of his gaze, to see the occupant of a
calash, daintily stepping out. Then, to her
horror, Louis was hurrying over to assist
her. True, it was an informal party, but
it was unpardonable that he should have
left her side for that woman! She dragged
her eyes away from them, speaking some
triviality to a near-by lady-in-waiting and
it was not until she heard Louis' voice

requesting to make the presentation, that she deigned to look at them.

"The Comtesse de Castiglione."

As the comtesse sank into her curtsy, Eugénie could barely repress a smile, for all that could be seen, was a huge cartwheel hat, trimmed with maribou feathers, but as she rose, the smile changed to a look of outraged dignity for the lady's dress was of the 'naked style' being fashioned in transparent muslin. Admittedly, some of her own friends favoured this daring style . . . but to wear such a dress for presentation!

She was instantly aware of the beautiful body, the immaculate shoulders and the small childlike face but she could never recall what words of welcome she spoke. At first, she felt a surge of relief when Louis, with Virginia on his arm strolled away, looking first at this flowering shrub . . . then that climbing rose but when he remained absent, leaving her alone, to receive their guests, a wave of anger swept over her, increasing to almost screaming point, when down by the lake-side, she saw him handing Virginia into a rowing-boat and he himself taking the oars.

She knew of the island in the middle of the lake; knew of its well-wooded sanctuary; the narrow, intimate, leafy-canopied paths; the grassy-carpeted boles of the trees. Already, she could visualise Virginia in Louis' arms.

She lay back in the luxuriously-cushioned chaise-longue, closing her eyes, the strains of the latest Strauss waltz mocking her senses. Louis and that strumpet would be humming it together as the music reached them over the water. Louis was clever. He knew all the sweet charming things a woman liked to hear. Tears pricked her eyes. Was it her fault that she thought physical love so degrading? Surely working for the advancement of the French Empire was far more rewarding.

Whenever she opened her eyes, there were couples strolling around, embracing as they walked, occasionally stopping to go into a still more clinging embrace, kissing with unrestrained passion. Usually it amused her to watch their amorous behaviour, just as she enjoyed listening to their stories of love-making. She knew that it was an odd quirk in her character

84

that she preferred to be a voyeuse rather than a participator, but tonight the whole scene sickened her.

She was roused by a sudden explosion, then a rushing, hissing sound. Great God! Another assassination? Here at Villeneuve l'Étang? Then she laughed in relief as a shower of multi-coloured stars fell from the skies. It was the beginning of the firework display.

One of her ladies approached. "Would you like your shawl, Madame? The evening is becoming cool."

She thought for a moment. "No, I think not, but I must confess to feeling somewhat weary. Perhaps a little supper, then I will retire."

Entering the lush-carpeted marquee, she was greeted by the popping of champagne corks, some of the guests already enjoying the delectable pâte-de-fois, chicken breasts, smoked salmon, strawberries and brandied cherries, petit-fours, peaches and pineapple, but at Eugénie's entrance they were on their feet as one.

Accompanied by her mother, Paca and the Duke of Alba she took her place at the raised table, but Louis' chair remained empty. The tables with their snow-white napery; the silver plate; the flower-filled vases, everything the epitomy of wealth and luxury was there. Yet in that bitter moment, it was all as naught to her. Everyone knew what had happened, but in Eugénie's hearing, none dare talk, though Mathilde and Plon-Plon who had joined them at the table, frequently exchanged smug glances. Plon-Plon had once been a suitor for Eugénie's hand and had been rejected in no uncertain manner. It would do her good to suffer a little ignominy . . .

She could not eat. Even the champagne appeared to have lost its sparkle. Outside, the banging, roaring and hissing continued, accompanied by squeals of delight and pretended fear. Louis and Virginia would be watching. Louis would be holding her close as she feigned childish alarm.

She could bear it no longer. Giving the signal to the Duc de Bassano, it was a relief to hear him announce that the Empress was about to retire and wished to bid her guests goodnight.

With ceremonious dignity the whole

assembly rose. There was dead silence in the marquee as they watched Eugénie make her bow, slow and deep; the gesture she had introduced at her very first assembly. They watched her raise her beautiful shoulders and then the imperious proud head, her eyes calm and serene as though defying all would be scoffers and gossips. Then she descended from the dais, daintily controlling the swaying of her crinoline as the gentlemen now bowed and the ladies sank into their curtsies.

Back in her room, however, she could not restrain her agitation, dismissing her woman ... she was waiting for the Emperor ... she would ring when she required her. How could she attempt to sleep when she was so full of anger?

She went to the window, her eyes straining over the lawns to the water's edge but despite the now thinning crowd, there was no sign of Louis.

She turned, startled as the door opened, to admit her mother and sister. Donna Manuela's voice was shrill. "It is disgraceful! Disgraceful! All Paris will be talking."

"Calm yourself, Mama." Paca turned to Eugénie, speaking quietly, "We thought you ought to know, Louis has driven into Paris . . . "

"With that . . . that . . . "

Paca nodded. "Don't distress yourself dear 'Gena. 'Tis but a passing fancy."

"Fancy!" Donna Manuela broke in, "He is her lover. Everyone knows that."

"Please Mama. Leave us. I will help 'Gena prepare for bed."

"It is my duty to comfort my child."

"No, Mama, no." Eugénie's voice was surprisingly cool and steady. "Paca is right. I would prefer you to go. We can talk in the morning."

"Dear Mother of God . . . to see my daughter, the Empress of France ousted by an Italian whore . . . "

"Mother!" Paca had taken her mother's arm and was propelling her through the door closing it with a sharp bang.

"Come 'Gena, shall I help you out of that crinoline or shall I ring for Pepa?"

"No, dear Paca. You stay. Do you think that woman is Louis' mistress?"

Paca hesitated. "Do any of us know when our husband takes a mistress?"

A look of amazement crossed Eugénie's face. "You don't think . . . you don't have any suspicion that James . . . your husband is unfaithful to you and has a mistress?"

"He is loving and kind both to me and the children, but what do I know of his private life? He travels on occasion without me. He frequently does not return home until the early hours of the morning but I do not torment myself as to whether he has a mistress."

"But everyone knows of Louis' affairs . . . "

"That is because he is the Emperor. The spies and agents enjoy spreading the gossip, hoping to disrupt the throne . . . "

"You are suggesting then, it is my duty to put on a brave face and behave as though I am the most beloved of wives . . . "

"And so you are. Oh 'Gena, you know you have the Emperor's love. Why can't you love him in return? Then . . . then, there would be none of . . . of . . . this . . . "

Eugénie suddenly laughed, almost lightheartedly. "Wouldn't there? Oh,

89

Paca, you are not so innocent that you are unaware of what is going on in the city . . . here at Court . . . everywhere. My ladies tell me many odd things — of the brothels for the middle-class — of the grand mansions occupied by courtesans made wealthy by their aristocratic lovers. They tell me of this duke who has set up a mistress in the rue de l'Arcade; another the lover of a courtesan who boasts several royal lovers. Plon-Plon, one mistress after another; Baron Haussmann actually driving in the Bois de Boulogne with a common actress . . . the duc de Morny . . . " Her voice was becoming shrill. "All of them, Paca . . . all of them . . . all our friends. Mistresses and lovers. All thinking they are being so discreet. Poor fools . . . poor fools."

"Yes, 'Gena, yes. They are fools. But now I am ringing for your maid. You need a hot, soothing drink, a sedative . . . and sleep."

★ ★ ★

Virginia Castiglione drew back the drapes to let in the morning light. From the bed, Louis watched her; grace in every movement, he thought. Then she slipped off the thin night robe, leaving her naked, bathed in the sunshine, standing poised like a white marble figurine. Louis drew in a sharp breath watching with admiration as she now picked up the filmy garment, dramatically holding it at arms' length, then folding it with exaggerated movements, at the same time, theatrically announcing, "This will be treasured with the greatest of care, until I again need it . . . as my shroud . . . for I shall leave instructions that I wish to be buried in it, being the robe I wore the first night I slept with the Emperor of France." She finished with a burst of hilarious laughter, in which Louis somewhat feebly joined, protesting. "Virginia, how can you have such morbid thoughts after last night? . . . "

"Because, at times, I am a morbid being, as you will find out. Now I am going to ring for breakfast. Was it not considerate, that my husband took himself away to Italy?"

★ ★ ★

The affair was becoming the talk of Paris for Louis was now spending every night with Virginia. He was having a suite of rooms prepared for her at the Élysee ... decorations ... new furniture. As a sop for the accommodating comte, Louis had given them a larger mansion, at 28 Avenue Montagne. Louis was completely besotted.

Whenever Eugénie spoke of their impending departure for Biarritz, he always had some ready, plausible excuse.

Donna Manuela continued to rave about the iniquity of her son-in-law. "Do you remember, Eugénie, how you dealt with him when you were first married and he continued to visit that Howard woman?"

As no answer was forthcoming, she went on, "You threatened to leave him; to return to Spain. He quickly came to heel. Why not repeat the threat?"

"No, Mama, no," interrupted Paca. "Such a threat would be useless, for neither the Emperor nor the Government would allow 'Gena to take the baby out of France. She turned to her sister, "Have patience, 'Gena."

"If only I could get him to Biarritz, away from the Comtesse, but he refuses to go."

When a few mornings later the message was brought that Louis was ill, she was all concern. Racing down to his apartments and joining the doctors at the bedside, she was appalled at the sight of Louis, his eyes, feverishly bright, his cheeks flushed and finding great difficulty with his breathing.

For a moment she continued to watch him, then whispered to the nearest doctor, "What is it, doctor? Is it dangerous?"

He indicated that they should move out of Louis' hearing, going over to the window, "Nothing, Your Majesty, that cannot be cured by rest and sleep."

"That woman," she thought angrily. "That woman." As though reading her thoughts, the doctor went on "His Majesty of late has been neglecting his health. Too many late hours; too little sleep. We shall insist he goes to Biarritz as soon as he is fit to travel." He smiled reassuringly at Eugénie, knowing only too well, of the inner torment she was enduring.

* * *

The gentle rhythm of the swaying train was as music to Eugénie's ears. They were actually on their way to Biarritz. The Imperial train, only recently presented to them by the Orleans Railway Company, was in itself a delight. Blue velvet curtains, lined with white silk, hung at windows and doors; sofas and chairs were upholstered in bright green silk, the same material lining the walls. The sleeping compartments, one transformed into a nursery for Lou-Lou, were all fitted out with every luxury.

Although it was now late August, there was still the expectancy of warm and good weather and the little sardine-fishing village of Biarritz had much to offer in the way of peace and solitude.

The white-shuttered Villa Eugénie had been Louis' gift to her the first summer of their marriage and it had been her delight to furnish it and plan the gardens which ran down a slope to their own private beach. Built high up on the cliffs, it commanded a wonderful view of beach, rocks and sea.

Louis' health was improving. He would put the Comtesse from his mind. The Court would not be returning direct to Paris, but to St. Cloud and then to Fontainbleu for the hunting season, and the masqued balls. There would be other beautiful women to distract him. She had no objection to his brief, flirtatious escapades; it was part of his very existence. He had once confessed to her "*Usually it is for the man to attack. As for me, I defend myself, but often I capitulate.*"

Tonight, their Imperial Majesties were the guests at a fancy-dress ball given by the Comte Walewski, recently appointed Minister of Foreign Affairs. The occasion was the opening of the Quai d'Orsay, and the natural son of the first Napoleon had spared no expense to impress the French Court. While in London as French Ambassador, his beautiful Florentine wife, Marie-Anne, had made a great impact on English society, Queen Victoria drawing her into the intimate royal circle, and now already finding great favour with Eugénie.

Seated on the raised dais, the Emperor

and Empress smilingly acknowledged new arrivals as they came forward to make their obeisance before being lost in the milling crowd, but, as usual, Eugénie's thoughts were veering in one direction. How soon would it be before the Castiglione arrived, not to set her heart pounding with jealousy, but to shame her as Empress of France.

After six weeks of blissful peace at Biarritz, she had returned to St. Cloud hopeful that the affair had died a natural death. Louis had been so considerate, making no demands. They had enjoyed the simple life, driving in the country, walking on the cliffs; picknicking on the beach. How they had delighted in watching the progress of Lou-Lou, watching him being bathed . . . pushing his pram along the garden paths. Her eyes took on a far-away look. Lou-Lou, although not yet a year old had already begun taking riding lessons. Much to Miss Shaw's horror, he was strapped on to a small Shetland pony, with Bachon, a groom in Louis' service, since days of exile, holding the leading rein, and shouting orders as though to a raw recruit on a barrack square. A son of hers and of Louis must be accomplished horseman.

It was with trepidation, however, that at the beginning of October, they returned to St. Cloud. Too soon her fears were realised, Louis almost immediately renewing the affair, visiting the comtesse every night, and as though he could not see sufficient of her during the night he now had the walls of each room of his apartment adorned by her portraits.

Christmas and the New Year had come and gone; Castiglione, along with her husband, being invited to Compiègne, then moving back to Paris to attend every ball and function. Eugénie would have found the situation more endurable had the Comtesse been of a more retiring nature.

Instead, she was blatantly impudent, deliberately flaunting the rules of Court, in such matters as wearing a straight dress, knowing that the crinoline was the accepted form for evening wear.

There was no other remedy than to ignore the creature.

She became aware that the music had stopped. Then an excited hub of chatter;

a scraping back of chairs and tables and then the amazing sight of guests, ladies and gentlemen alike clambering onto furniture to watch the entry of the Comtesse de Castiglione. As usual, her dress was of almost transparent material, golden in colour, the skirts a little fuller than usual, but it was the form of trimming that held all viewers spell-bound. Appearing as the Queen of Hearts, she had chains of jewelled hearts placed in certain positions to deliberately rouse comment. Brazenly she stared up at the Empress before making her curtsy, so that Eugénie, who never spoke to her, could not refrain from a very caustic "You wear your heart very low, do you not Madame?"

As usual the woman's presence left her feeling angry and frustrated, but tonight she felt even more apprehensive. Someone had set the rumour circulating that Virginia was with child. Commonsense told her that it could be Louis' child, but how could he bring such disgrace to the throne?"

He was so maddening, so baffling. He would come to her each morning to ask her opinion or advice on some state matter. He would listen to what she had to say, often heeding her advice. He was generous. He denied her nothing. At the present moment, a magnificent mansion was being built for Paca; a Parisian palace for all future Dukes of Alba.

Louis suddenly rose, and without a word, followed the Comtesse. It was the same pattern on every occasion. Only recently while at the theatre, Virginia had pleaded a headache, and left early. For a while the Emperor fidgeted about in the Royal Box, then he too made his exit, leaving Eugénie the cynosure of all curious and amused eyes.

Mme Walewska was all sympathy, but after all, she said, Louis was a Napoleon. Was not her husband the result of an illicit Napoleonic affair? As for the Comtesse, the Emperor would eventually tire of her. Why, did the Empress not know, how universally disliked the creature was? Did she not know that her own ladies refused to serve her with tea and cakes; ignoring and passing her by?

Eugénie had laughed. "Of course I

know — and I've seen what happens."

"Happens, Your Majesty?"

"The Comtesse merely goes up to some innocent guest, and calmly takes her plate, with a casual 'You don't mind if I have this do you?' Ah, she's an impudent one is the Comtesse."

★ ★ ★

Virginia Castiglione cast a final glance round the lavishly furnished boudoir. Everything was in readiness; the big fire; the wine table set out with glasses, wine and brandy and the inevitable silver box of cigarettes. Louis was late. He usually arrived about eleven-thirty, and it was now approaching midnight. Pray God, he didn't fail to come. Cavour was pressing for more information; more vital information. Was it her fault that the Emperor preferred to make love rather than discuss state affairs? Now Cavour was threatening that unless she made more progress, she would be replaced. That must not happen. Louis was such a generous lover, giving her vast sums of money for beautiful clothes; exquisite furniture and paintings; unexpected gifts of priceless jewellery. No, she couldn't afford to lose Louis. *Her mother should have never married her to Castiglione. Had she brought her to France, no Spanish woman would have reigned there.*

Now she didn't care what became of the throne of France. In addition to working for Italy she was also passing on information to the Duc d'Aurnole, Orleanist pretender to the throne. She was enjoying the excitement of this game of intrigue.

Often, though still in the early hours of the morning, she would order her carriage immediately on Louis' departure, and with information fresh in her mind drive off to a secret rendezvous to meet Cavour, or one of his agents.

Then back home to bed until it was time to dress for her drive down the Bois de Boulogne in the splendid new carriage . . . a present from Louis, with the powdered footmen up behind to enjoy the admiration of the gaping crowds along the roadside; sometimes to hear the vulgar derision of those who recognised her as the 'Emperor's whore'. She enjoyed it all.

She began to be anxious. Perhaps Louis was not coming tonight. Perhaps he was angry about her latest naughtiness. Perhaps that ill-tempered wife of his was railing at him about it. She had actually created, when she, Virginia, had worn a crown, fashioned in feathers. Yet, she was important. There were those at Court who feared to offend her, lest their positions became insecure. Had she not been accustomed since childhood, to being named as 'God's most exquisite creation?'

There was an indistinct murmur of voices outside the door. God be praised, he had arrived . . . apparently as usual with his equerry, Comte Fleury and a policeman! It amused her to think of Fleury in an adjoining room . . . the policeman down below . . . and the coachmen huddled up on the driving seat of the Emperor's waiting coach.

As Louis entered the room, she mockingly dropped him a curtsy, before throwing herself into his arms, but as he led her towards the sofa, she was quick to note that he almost immediately released himself.

"You are angry with me," she pouted.

"It was unpardonable, Virginia . . . an insult to the Empress, and I will not have her . . ."

"An insult to copy her hair style? I always thought, imitation was the sincerest form of flattery?"

"It was not imitation. It was downright unmitigated theft . . ."

"What has she told you?"

"She asked her hairdresser to design a special coiffure for this evening . . . something new . . . different. Somehow, this intelligence reached your ears and you so worked on the poor fellow as to betray the style, on your solemn oath that you had no intention of copying the Empress. But there you were, the very same arrangement of curls, feathers, jewels. It was a cruel, spiteful trick. Can you not understand the Empress' anger and humiliation?"

"Poor Louis. Your Empress has no sense of humour."

"I fail to see any humour in underhand behaviour . . ."

"I am sorry. I will apologise to her Majesty."

"I think it would be wiser to stay away from Court for the next few days until she has cooled down."

She took a cigarette from the box, lit it and handed it to him. As he noticed the long, delicate fingers, the scarlet lips, pouting like a naughty child, he almost felt ashamed of his anger.

The cigarette was relaxing as was the gentle way she stroked his beard, curled her fingers round his moustache, so that soon they were locked in a close embrace, all anger spent. It was not until several hours later, that a discreet knock on the door roused them. It was Fleury, reminding his master of the approach of dawn, the necessity to return to the Tuileries, while there were few people abroad.

There were long, clinging embraces, a whispered "Until tonight, *mon amour*." A quick kiss "Au revoir *ma perle*," and Louis was following Fleury down the staircase out into the April morning.

Neither spoke as they took their seats in the coupé, and the policeman climbed up beside the coachman. Then it happened. From some point of concealment, three men dashed out and made a grab for the horses. Louis' first instinctive thought was assassination, but the coachman was quick to act, using his whip with telling effect on the attackers, until they had to release their hold, and he could speed up the horses back to the Tuileries.

Inside the coupé, Louis was first to speak. "This affair must be kept quiet. No harm has been done. I want no arrests — no prosecution."

"But, sir," Fleury protested, "Cannot you see your life is in constant danger. For a long time, you have been warned that there have been leakages concerning your movements . . . "

"But I cannot have the lady's name involved . . . "

"Discretion can be employed, sir, but the culprits must be apprehended."

Back in the Palace, the policeman too, assured his Majesty, that he must report the incident, reluctant though he was. Louis shrugged his shoulders in resignation. Was it getting too dangerous to go out without an armed escort . . . even in the search of love?

★ ★ ★

Acting on the advice of the Chief of Police, Louis stayed away from the Rue de Montagne during the next few days, in the course of which three Italians were arrested, one Tibaldi, confessing that he was in the pay of Mazzini, the head of an Italian secret society, now living as an exile in London.

Eugénie could not restrain her anger and disgust. "Perhaps now you can see the evil in the woman. She it was . . . there was none other to betray you . . . she would have had you killed . . ."

"Nonsense. She is perfectly innocent. There would be many who knew of my comings and goings."

"To your shame, sir. Yes. And what of this other rumour that is circulating through the salons? . . ."

"There are always rumours. To which do you refer?"

She almost spat out the word. "That your mistress is with child."

106

For a moment a look of alarm showed in his eyes, then with false unconcern, "She is a married lady. Why should she not have a child? She has certainly not informed me of the possibility."

"You know full well, the possibility is, it could be your child." Her anger suddenly gave way, first to hysterical weeping and then screaming. "Oh, how I loathe you. How I loathe all men."

★ ★ ★

Louis was calling on Virginia in full daylight, risking no lurking assassins. She was well aware of the reason why Louis had neglected her, for by now all Paris knew of the affair; the newspapers being full of varied and exaggerated accounts.

At Louis' request, the Police had refused to divulge the address, merely referring to the case as No. 28, but all the salons knew that Louis had been with Virginia Castiglione: and what the salons knew one day, it was common knowledge the next.

The Police also had a request to make. That the Comtesse should be asked to leave Paris. As kindly as he could for he hated hurting any woman, he told Virginia of the Police decree, expecting tears and pouts, but as he watched, her face grew stony and hard, her eyes like small black pebbles, first lifeless, then taking on a cunning grin.

"If then, I am to leave Paris, where would you wish your child to be born?"

For a moment he felt as though she had struck him. "Virginia . . . it can't be . . . you are married . . . the comte . . . "

"It could be his child . . . or . . . it could be yours . . . "

"Virginia," his voice had taken on a pleading tone. "There must be no scandal. Whether his child or mine . . . I will provide . . . for both you and the child."

She suddenly laughed. "Poor Louis. You are afraid. Well, money and position can cover up most transgressions . . . but do not keep me out of France too long."

6

AS Eugénie followed the footman from room to room through the Emperor's apartments, instructing him to remove from the walls all portraits of Virginia Castiglione, her spirits soared high. Louis had made no demur when she told him of her intention. On the contrary, as she told her ladies amidst much light-hearted chatter, he seemed relieved to be rid of the reminders.

"Well, that's understandable, Madame," broke in Marie Walewska, "seeing that he had already begun to tire of her."

"What gives you cause to think that?" There was curiosity in Eugénie's voice.

Expressively shrugged shoulders preceded the artless reply. "Why, Madame? Simply because the Emperor himself told me so." Then seeing the puzzled frown on Eugénie's face, added consolingly, "You see, Madame, he had to confide in someone and with the gulf between you, he naturally turned to me, your

109

dearest friend . . . "

Was the time now opportune to make a fresh beginning with her husband? As she repeatedly told herself, there was so much about Louis, she did admire. She sighed deeply. Yes. The next time Louis visited her room, she would not repulse him. Noticing the Empress' distraction, Marie Walewska asked, with a hint of amusement in her voice, "Have you any more news concerning Her Majesty, Queen Victoria?"

Instantly, Eugénie's eyes lit up. "Why, yes. I had a letter this morning, written by the Queen herself."

"Is she progressing favourably?"

"Indeed, she is . . . already anxious to leave her bed."

"And the baby?"

"Like all Her Majesty's other babies, no trouble at all. They have already chosen her names. The first is to be Beatrice."

Marie Walewska could not contain her mirth. "But nine . . . nine children."

"To go through that ordeal nine times," Eugénie was murmuring, almost inaudibly.

"But she finds childbirth easy, Madame, especially now with the much vaunted chloroform," but Eugénie's thoughts had transferred themselves to the connubial bliss that Victoria and Albert must share, both on the same emotional and physical plane. Would to God, she and Louis were more evenly matched.

When just after their return from Biarritz last year, Victoria had written she was again pregnant, there had been much bawdy comment as to Albert's prowess and Victoria's highly-sexed nature, obviously inherited from her Hanoverian ancestors. They were wrong. The baby was the result of their mutual love.

Mentally, she shook herself. "As you know, it is already arranged the Emperor and I are visiting Her Majesty at Osborne in August. In the meantime, now I know all is well with her and the baby, will you send off the silk peignoir, I recently chose for her. She so admired those I wore during our mornings together."

Despite all her good intentions, Eugénie could find no pleasure in lovemaking. On the contrary, there were times when it left her irritable and bad-tempered. Perhaps all the gossip and rumours circulating concerning Virginia Castiglione were adding to her confusion; gossip that the Comtesse had given birth to a son; rumour which said the Count had refused to acknowledge paternity and that the Comtesse had no wish to be encumbered with a child. So, continued rumour, she had brought the baby back to France to be reared by French foster-parents.

Eugénie could not bring herself to make enquiries as to the truth. She preferred to remain in ignorance as to the child's whereabouts. Knowing of Louis' great love for children she was well aware, that through reliable friends, he would have made adequate provision.

The hurt however persisted. That Louis could have taken a mistress and fathered another son, so soon after Lou-Lou's birth, bewildered her.

It therefore carne as a relief when he relaxed his visits to her apartments, for oddly enough, a warmer relationship then appeared to develop between them. She knew of course, that Bachiocci, the Emperor's *maitre de plaisir*, would be arranging assignments with certain females, but she felt no jealousy in that matter. Castiglione had gone.

As the time of their visit to England drew near, she began to have doubts concerning their welcome. She questioned Marie Walewska as to how the Queen would regard the Castiglione affair, knowing the rigidity of her court.

Marie had laughed. "'Tis not the Queen, so much, Madame, but the Prince. He is the stiff, stern upholder of the morals. Yet, unknown to him, there are many of the Queen's statesmen who have taken mistresses and quite a few of her ladies boast a lover, but they are discreet and take care not to be discovered."

Of course Victoria would know all about the attack on Louis; the English papers had made much of the case which was to come up for hearing immediately on their return.

She was looking forward to the visit with two-fold anticipation; first to discuss their respective babies and secondly to help the Princess Royal choose her trousseau, now her engagement to Crown

Prince Frederick of Prussia had been announced, the marriage to take place in the New Year.

Yet from the moment she and Louis greeted their hosts, she sensed a change in the atmosphere. Albert was still the very correct, punctilious Prussian, only now, a shade still more remote but it was in Victoria's attitude towards Louis, the censure was so obvious, giving him no encouragement for any flirtatious overture. There was even a change in her regard for Eugénie, a motherly, unspoken sympathy, 'You poor, brave, ill-treated little wife.'

Disregarding the coolness, Louis appeared to be quite happy to plod around after Albert, inspecting his model farm comparing it with his at Biarritz, leaving the ladies to indulge in their chatter and intimate talks.

"I had hoped to see the baby princess," ventured Eugénie at the first opportunity.

A mouè of distaste crossed Victoria's florid face, "Oh no. I do not like small babies. I prefer them when they begin to walk and talk. In any case, a baby of four months is too young to travel. I was hoping to see the Prince Imperial," she finished laughingly.

"We did consider bringing him but decided it would not be wise to uproot him for so short a while." She paused and then went on excitedly, "He can both walk and talk . . . and so very intelligent." As Victoria made no comment, she continued, "Whenever he accompanies me in my carriage, he wears the full uniform of the Imperial Guards, standing on my knee, imitating their marching and acknowledging salutes."

Victoria smiled knowingly. It was so natural . . . and forgivable to enthuse over the first baby. When Eugénie added more to her nursery, she wouldn't have a bouncing eighteen-month-old accompanying her on afternoon drives.

Although now about to marry, Vicky could not restrain her girlish adoration for Eugénie . . . and her beautiful clothes, turning to her for advice on latest styles and materials.

Together, the three of them pored over the fashion journals, some of which Eugénie had brought from Paris but the Queen shook her head at most of the styles favoured by her daughter.

"No, Vicky, no. Such styles would not be suitable for a German princess. The German ladies are more restrained; less décolletée and though Papa and I wish to give you a trousseau worthy of your high rank, yet such expensive materials, so much lace and braid would offend the German court."

"But Vicky is young. Some day, she will be the Empress of Germany. Would it not be to her distinction if she were to introduce new styles, to become a leader of fashion?" Eugénie's voice was soft and coaxing.

Victoria shook her head determinedly. "Never. Her Papa would be outraged to see her in some of those dresses." She indicated those displayed in the French journals. "Your Parisian ladies may favour these, but . . . " With a toss of her head, she left the sentence unfinished. When Eugénie found herself alone with Vicky, she consoled, "I have already ordered a dress for you from my dressmaker. It is of lace, *points d'Alencon*, with many flounces and my favourite bunches of violets."

116

Vicky flung her arms around Eugenie. "I know it will be the most beautiful dress of all. Oh, thank you, dear Aunt Eugenie, thank you." There was a pause and then, half laughing, half crying, she went on, "Do you know, Mama has provided me with twenty pairs of goloshes and scores and scores of sponges . . . "

Sweet seventeen, thought Eugénie whimsically; longing for silks and lace and Mama thinking in terms of dry feet and clean skins.

The four days passed swiftly; uneventful pleasant days spent in the open air. Restful, cosy evenings playing cards and singing round the piano. Friends entertaining friends.

Not once, did either Victoria or Albert mention the name of Castiglione or the attack on Louis.

★ ★ ★

They stayed in Paris until the trial was over, Tibaldi being sentenced to transportation for life, but both Louis and Eugénie well aware of the danger that remained, for Mazzini, the exiled Italian and instigator, had the temerity to write, "*The execution of the attempt on Napoleon is a vital thing for Italy.*"

Then they were away to Biarritz to enjoy the simple life once again; Lou-Lou playing on the sands with his cousins, Carlos, Marquinita and Chiquita; long, warm, lazy days in the company of dear Paca; a family gathering with Donna Manuela dominating the scene and not even Louis taking any offence whatever she said or did.

All too soon, the return to Paris, St. Cloud and Compiègne in readiness for the Christmas festivities, where the house-parties would number over a hundred guests and the attendance at the masked balls and banquets would reach into thousands.

It was at the opening house-party that the first note of suspicion was whispered to Eugénie. It had been a mad, chaotic evening, dancing to a barrel-organ, singing bawdy songs and playing childish games.

It was during a game of blind-man's buff, with Louis blind-fold, that Prosper

Mérimée drew Eugénie's attention to the game.

"Odd, is it not," he remarked dryly, "how many times Mme. Walewska deliberately puts herself in the Emperor's path?"

"She does appear to be in a frivolous mood this evening . . . "

"But do they need to make their kisses so long and lingering?"

She looked up sharply. "What are you inferring?"

He sighed. He had known Eugénie since the early days of her childhood; knew of the many heart-aches she had experienced and here was another about to overtake her.

"I do not trust Mme. Walewska . . . "

"Nonsense. She is my closest friend."

"She is also becoming the Emperor's closest friend . . . "

"No. No. I do not believe it," but deep down as she watched Louis and Marie stroll away, their arms entwined, she knew. Mons. Mérimée was right.

She spent a sleepless night. How was she going to face this new danger . . . if danger there was? Prosper Mérimée was a veritable old gossip, but she had to find out.

She decided she would ask Louis outright, going down to his apartments shortly before lunch. Reaching the foot of the staircase, she was amazed to see Louis and Marie in a close embrace outside his bedroom door. Quickly, to avoid being seen, she stepped into his study, glad of the opportunity to regain her composure, not leaving the room until she thought the way was clear.

Outside the door, she almost collided with the lady herself and to her discomfort, it was she who was embarrassed, not Marie.

"I . . . I am looking for the Emperor," she stammered.

"Then I regret I cannot help you Madame. I have not seen him this morning."

There was no need to ask Louis. Mme. Walewska had told her. The deliberate lie was full confirmation she was Louis' mistress.

The succession of entertaining, first at one royal residence, then another was a long drawn-out torture for Eugénie for it seemed everyone else had known the position for some time; everyone at Court accepting Madame Walewska as the new *Maîtresse de Titre* . . . even Count Walewska.

During those miserable weeks, Eugénie came to a decision. She couldn't dismiss Marie from Court . . . Louis would forbid it. Let the affair take its course. There would always be a *Maîtresse de Titre*, she told herself bitterly. She would be civil to her, causing no scandal. At least, she would be preserving her pride.

The New Year had been ushered in and they had returned to The Tuileries. Tonight, she and Louis were attending a gala performance at the Opera, an occasion for the public to enjoy the spectacle of the Cent-Gardes as escort to Their Majesties; the spectacle being enhanced by the forest of gas-lamps adding to the brilliancy of their swords and cuirasses.

Despite the cold January night, crowds had massed along the route, cheering themselves hoarse as the royal carriage approached and passed, enabling them to catch but little more than the gleam of Eugénie's diamonds.

Nearing the theatre, the coachman slackened the pace of his horses, while the excited crowd pressed forward, attempting to break the cordons, hoping to see the Emperor and Empress leave their coach.

Then, without warning, there was a sudden, blinding flash, a deafening roar and the roadway was plunged into darkness.

The coach came to a standstill but before either Louis or Eugénie could speak or act, another roaring explosion added to the confusion almost drowning the anguished cries of the injured and the terrifying whinnying of the horses.

Amidst the darkness and chaos, Eugénie became aware there were men endeavouring to wrench open the doors. This then was the end. Visions of Marie Antoinette and her ladies flashed across her mind, yet she felt no cringing fear.

Another violent explosion. The men at the doors were using even greater force to get them open and as they finally did so, she hit out at them with her fan, "I am the Empress. Take your hands away."

"Your pardon, Your Majesty. We are the police escort. Allow us to help you into the theatre."

She felt a surge of relief but now that lamps had been produced, she could see the bleeding and distorted bodies of men and women lying on the footpaths. The realisation that these people were dead and dying; innocent people when she and Louis had been the intended victims filled her with horror and remorse and turning to her rescuers, said, *"Don't bother about us. Such things are our profession. Look after the wounded,"* yet when Louis would have remained, feeling it was his duty to stay, she seized his arm, hurrying him into the theatre, hissing, *"Don't be stupid."*

Inside the foyer, they were surrounded by well-wishers congratulating them on their miraculous escape for neither Louis nor Eugénie had more than minute facial scratches. As they entered their box, the audience rose as one, the auditorium resounding again and again with their cheers. She smiled and waved in acknowledgement; false smile to reassure the people the Bonaparte monarchy would never submit to violence, yet throughout the whole performance, she heard naught of the music for it was drowned by the memory of the awful shrieks and screaming amidst the explosion of bombs. Would the opera never end? She wanted to be out among the injured to comfort her people instead of sitting there on a gilded, velvet-upholstered chair.

At last the ordeal was over and they were driving back to the Tuileries, followed by a stream of cheering citizens, thankful their Emperor and Empress had survived the assassination.

Only when she and Louis were alone, did her calm give way. Ten people dead and one hundred and forty injured. It was monstrous. The villains must be caught.

The police had no difficulty in making arrests, the chief of whom was an Italian, Felice Orsini. The French people, however were not satisfied. It was very quickly brought to light, the bombs had been made in England. What was more, all the arrested men had recently come over from England, where they had been living in exile. Obviously, stormed the French newspapers, the assassins were receiving help and encouragement from the English government. The English press was quick to retort and the verbal warfare rapidly gathered momentum, despite Louis' protests, no blame should be attached to England.

Victoria had lost no time in expressing her sympathy at the dastardly attack but Eugénie feared the violence of the French newspapers would bring about a rupture in their friendship.

She had already sent gifts for Vicky's imminent wedding; the promised dress and several pieces of jewellery. On the night of the wedding, the English ambassador was giving a banquet in honour of the newly-weds with Louis and Eugénie as the principal guests. Both the government and press urged they should not attend so soon after the attempt on their lives but the Emperor and Empress were adamant. They would most certainly grace the happy occasion; they had no wish to offend Victoria and Albert.

At the end of the assassination trial,

Eugénie was deeply distressed when she heard all three men had been sentenced to the guillotine.

"You must uphold their appeal, Louis. Use your prerogative for mercy . . . "

He shook his head. "Twill be of little use, chérie. So many Frenchmen died that night; so many more maimed and crippled for the rest of their lives . . . "

" . . . And more will die and be maimed if we make martyrs of these men. Send them out of the country and they will quickly be forgotten."

"You are right but my pleas for leniency are viewed abroad with suspicion . . . especially in England."

When Orsini's wife sought an audience to plead for her husband's life, Eugénie broke down and wept along with her, but no purpose was served. The government was determined the ultimate penalty must be paid, threatening, if Louis insisted on using his prerogative, they would resign en bloc.

Realising the possible far-reaching troubles such an event could incur, Louis had no alternative but to capitulate.

7

PROSPER MÉRIMÉE was still warning her about Marie Walewska. "Eugénie, I beg of you be more discreet; more discerning what you say when she is near . . . "

"But why? Providing I am speaking the truth . . . "

"But she does not. You are too honest . . . too outspoken. She has a way of dissembling your words; twisting your statements, both to the Emperor himself and to the various diplomats who visit the Foreign Office."

She gave a short, mocking laugh. "Your reputation, as a gossip, dear Prosper, does not diminish."

"Nor does my observance and hearing. Believe me, Eugénie, she is far more dangerous than Castiglione ever was."

"But what can I do?" There was a wail of desperation in the query.

"As I said before, do not be drawn into any discussion concerning state

127

affairs . . . not even with your other ladies, for I know she quizzes them." He suddenly changed the topic of their conversation. "Will Mme. Walewska be accompanying you and the Emperor on your tour of Brittany?"

Her eyes hardened. "You should know the Emperor never goes far without her."

"And the meeting at Cherbourg with Queen Victoria? Will Mme. Walewska be in the party?"

"Indeed, yes. She and the Queen were great friends when the Count was ambassador in London. Is it not droll, Monsieur, that her Majesty will be greeting both wife and mistress?" She forced a laugh but Prosper Mérimée could detect the nearness of tears.

★ ★ ★

Cherbourg harbour was gay with bunting, union-jack and tri-colour hanging side by side from every vantage point. Bands on the quay-side played bravely on, despite the regular interruptions from the guns of French battleships, proudly riding at anchor, greeting the arrival of the royal yacht, *Victoria and Albert*.

As Eugénie and Louis, followed by their ladies and gentlemen went aboard, Queen Victoria and Prince Albert stood unsmilingly awaiting them.

Immediately Eugénie sensed impending disaster but with feigned imperturbability, went towards them, to be rewarded by Victoria's dour features momentarily relaxing into a smile as the two ladies embraced, only to be replaced by a near scowl as she greeted Louis.

Now Eugénie was presenting her ladies, the Queen kissing each on the cheek as she rose from her obeisance. As they approached Marie Walewski, Eugénie bit her lip. The ignominy of it, that Victoria should be a witness of her humiliation. Then the unexpected happened, the Queen deliberately ignoring Mme. Walewska, passing her by as though she didn't exist. Not a taffeta skirt or petticoat dared to rustle, but Eugénie's heart leaped with joy to think that she still had the Queen's sympathy and friendship.

Nevertheless the atmosphere was tense; the conversation stilted until Victoria essayed bluntly, "France is increasing her naval armaments, is she not, sir?"

"Yes, Your Majesty. A strong navy is a country's first line of defence."

She regarded him with severity. "You are not expecting war, are you sir?"

Louis smiled urbanely. "Indeed not, Madam, and while France can boast the finest navy in Europe, she has no fear of such an event."

Eugénie flinched under the cross-barrage of unfriendly speech only too glad to take her leave and return to the battleship *La Bretagne*, where that evening, she was giving a dinner party for the royal visitors, but it was a dinner-party matted by an alien atmosphere of suspicion and mistrust; but blessed by the absence of the Walewskis who had been instructed that their presence was not required.

Mercifully the two-day visit quickly passed, both parties being glad to make their farewells, farewells without any tears or distress.

★ ★ ★

Their stay in Biarritz that year was the most disappointing that Eugénie could recall.

When Louis informed her that the Walewski family was accompanying them, she almost decided to remain in Paris, but Lou-Lou and Miss Shaw had already gone ahead. Why should she deny herself of her little son's company, but when Plon-Plon suddenly arrived, she felt her Paradise had been invaded by a nest of vipers.

Paca did her best to restore her calm but the day came, when even she began to understand her sister's dilemma. They were sitting on the verandah, idly watching, with the aid of binoculars, any ship that hove in sight; occasionally scanning the beach to watch the comings and goings of the children, when Eugénie gave a sudden exclamation of surprise. "Look, Paca. On the beach. The three people walking together."

Paca recognised them immediately. The Emperor and his cousin, Prince Napoleon and between them, Marie Walewska, all talking in an animated, excited manner.

"It is obvious, is it not, that Plon-Plon has come here to discuss some important matter. But why is Marie Walewska with them?" Eugénie's voice was full of agitation.

Paca lowered her binoculars. "Perhaps we are making a mountain out of a molehill," she comforted. "Mme. Walewska is a woman who enjoys male company and flattery . . ."

"And intrigue. Plon-Plon has not come here to enjoy the sea breezes. He is up to some mischief and Marie Walewski is helping to stir the witches' brew . . ."

For the remainder of the stay in Biarritz, she found herself watching. It seemed that the trio were for ever in earnest conversation; conversation from which she was excluded.

The conspiracy of whispering followed them back to the Tuileries, St. Cloud and on to Compiègne.

A stag-hunt had been arranged, but from the November skies, a continuous downpour put the day's sport out of the question. Eugénie was not sorry. A large house-party had gathered, but now, this morning, she could keep to her room until lunch-time.

She would have breakfast in bed and then read her letters, and morning papers. There was a cheerful fire, in the grate and because of the gloom, the gas-lighting was full on. It was a morning to be enjoyed.

Pepa removed the breakfast tray, plumped up the pillows and handed her mistress the morning papers; an inscrutable look in her eyes. The Empress was a good mistress handing to her all cast-off gowns to do with what she would. Already she was building up a sizeable bank-account by their sale to American ladies. Would she be pleased by this morning's surprising news?

The words blazoned themselves across the width of the paper. PRINCE NAPOLEON TO MARRY. Eugénie read and re-read them in amazement. Then she was scanning the smaller print, going back to read it again to get the full import. She felt her skin prickling. The bride was to be Princess Clothilde, sixteen-year-old daughter of the King of Italy. How could the King give his daughter to the ugly, lecherous forty-six-year-old roué, who flaunted one mistress after another?

But it was what she next read that caused her to pull the bed-side bell with such urgency that brought Pepa hastening back into the room.

"I have changed my mind. I wish to dress. Hurry. Hurry."

How dare he treat her as though she was some unimportant, distant member of the family . . . somebody of no concern.

Louis was already at work in his study, looking up in amazement as Eugénie burst in . . . She held the newspaper out to him. "Why wasn't I told about this? Why did I have to learn it from a newspaper? Not that I am interested in what that imbecile does . . . save that I pity the poor child. No. It is the other things which I read. That you had a secret meeting with Count Cavour, as far back as last July, when you allied yourself with Italy in case of war. That is what you discussed at Biarritz was it not? You and your warmongering cousin and the Italian Walewska. A war in exchange for a sixteen-year-old princess, and I wasn't told, because you knew I should tell you not to be such a fool; that France is in no position to go to war ... she would lose the friendship of the rest of Europe. But she was told ... she was in the secret ... " Her voice was reaching a high pitch and she had to pause to regain her breath, Louis seizing the opportunity to gently seat her in a chair.

"No, Eugénie no. That was not the reason. I have no fears for France ... "

"Then why was I not told? Surely as the Empress of France ... "

"Listen, Eugénie. Listen. The meeting with Cavour took place just before the visit of Queen Victoria to Cherbourg. I was afraid that in your conversation with the Queen ... you might ... "

"Go on. You were afraid that I might ... might what?"

"Eugénie, ma chéri, your greatest fault is that you are too impulsive ... too indiscreet ... that you get carried away in conversation ... "

"In other words, that I talk too much? That I am not to be trusted?"

"Please, Eugénie, try to understand . . . "

"I understand only too clearly. The Italian whore is to be trusted. I am not. It is you who do not understand. Had I been informed of the secret and asked to keep silent, do you think I would have betrayed you?"

"No. No, but at the time, the matter was so urgent, I was afraid . . . "

"Afraid? You, a Bonaparte afraid?" There was bitter sarcasm in her voice. "From the newspaper," she went on. "I read that an agreement was reached whereby France will go to the aid of Italy in case of war. Is there going to be a war, sir?"

He made a gesture of weariness. "I do not know. Italy wishes to be rid of the Austrians from her northern provinces."

"Then let Italy fight her own wars. Why should Frenchmen give their lives for Italy?"

"It is too late now. France has given her word . . . "

She rose from the chair, anger blaring in her eyes, "Then God help France . . . and you . . . " and without a further glance at him left the room.

The Italian royal wedding had taken place amidst great pomp and ceremony, and now, the bride was making her first obeisance to Eugénie, and meeting the Parisian Court. Eugénie's first impression was that of a very plain-faced child, but when she asked her to be seated by her side, while she presented her ladies, she was greatly surprised by her poise and graciousness. Obviously she had been well schooled. Pray God, Cousin Mathilde would be kind to this very young, new sister-in-law.

* * *

Louis was in a fever of excitement. Men and women, arms linked were marching up and down the cherry-blossomed boulevards, singing the Marseillaise, suppressed by the first Emperor Napoleon, but now revived with unbelievable enthusiasm as its sanguinary dictates invaded every restaurant and café.

France had declared war on Austria, and on that beautiful May morning of

1859, their Emperor, fully equipped in battledress had ridden away to join his troops, his final message to the country being *'France has not drawn the sword to conquer but to liberate.'*

Eugénie had experienced a complete change of heart regarding the war, for, during Louis' absence, she was to be Regent of France, the prospect filled her with elation. Power had been the motivation of her marriage. So far, she had had no opportunity to prove her capabilities, but now she had the rein in her hands.

Three times a week she presided over her Cabinet, first studying reports from all parts of France and Europe, including those from the war zone, enabling her to discuss important matters with ease and confidence.

Within three weeks, Louis had scored a victory at the Battle of Magenta. Unable to contain her jubilation she and Princess Clothilde drove down the Rue de Rivoli and through the flower bedecked boulevards, to a crescendo of cheering and a continuous rendering of the Marseillaise.

Then came the cold-water douche. At the outbreak of the war Victoria had written, *'should Louis himself invade Austrian possessions, it would be only natural if Germany, alarmed to see one of the most important members of the Confederation attacked, and in danger, were to come to Austria's aid . . .'*

Now, despite the victory, Eugénie began to feel alarmed, for the news was conveyed to her that Prussia was mobilising and that Victoria's son-in-law, Crown Prince Frederick was to be in command of the Prussian Infantry.

Hastily, she wrote Louis, asking that she might visit him to discuss certain important matters, but with equal speed, back came his terse reply. As Regent, she could not leave France.

There was nothing she could do but watch and wait, but before the month was out, came the Battle of Solferino, another resounding victory for Louis.

Bursting with joy and jubilation, she immediately ordered a Te Deum to be sung at Notre Dame to be followed by general rejoicing in the brilliantly lit squares and boulevards.

But there were the wives and mothers who went to Notre Dame, not to rejoice, but to pray for the safe homecoming of their men-folk, for rumour brought news, that the slaughter on both sides had been horrific.

Eugénie's exultation was soon overtaken by increased anxiety, for the mutterings in Europe were growing. Surely now, the Austrians should recognise defeat? Finally, in a mood of desperation, she sent a coded message to the Emperor, suggesting he should negotiate an armistice, warn of Prussia's mobilisation; England's antagonism, and the general feeling of horror towards modern warfare.

★ ★ ★

Without waiting to be announced, Count Cavour burst into Marie Walewska's sitting-room, anger written across his swarthy face.

"You've led us into a fine impasse, Madame . . . two months of war, and the gallant Napoleon is already negotiating peace terms."

She regarded him with hauteur, "Are

you attaching the blame to me?"

"I am, Madame, I am. You were left in Paris to watch the Empress. She it is who has badgered him . . . letters . . . telegrams . . . Why did you not intercept them?"

"I did not know of them. In any case they would be in secret code."

"You could have discovered them . . . had them decoded. That was your task . . ."

"There was no opportunity. The Empress suddenly became so high and mighty . . . speaking to no-one . . . as close as a clam . . ."

Striding about the room, striking his fists into the palms of his hands, his voice became belligerent. "Two victories . . . then seeking peace. I will not stand for it. It is a violation of the agreement we made at Plombières last July. I shall resign, and if I go down, Madame, I will take others with me."

Marie winced. If her husband lost office, it would mean farewell to Court. Probably her dismissal as *maîtresse de titre*.

★ ★ ★

141

Eugénie was shocked at the appearance of the returning all-conquering Emperor. In the space of a few months he seemed to have aged several years.

"You must see a doctor, Louis. You are ill."

"No. No. 'Tis nothing time cannot cure. It is the memory of Solferino. The carnage, it was terrible. Truly, our artillery was magnificent, but it was nothing more than mass slaughter and inhuman suffering. The sooner we get away to Biarritz, the sooner the horror will fade from my memory."

"Poor Louis! But we have to remain in Paris until all the troops have returned. I have arranged a military review in their honour . . . and, of course, certain victory celebrations."

The review was intended to be a grand military spectacle; thousands of troops on parade with hundreds of cannons trundling in their wake, but with the combined excitement of the crowds and the exuberance of the returning soldiers, it became more of a riotous carnival procession.

In full uniform, the three-year-old

Prince Imperial was seated before his father on his charger, doing his share of the shouting and yelling. The colourful Zouaves created wild enthusiasm as they waved their red-tasselled caps atop their muskets, Louis himself joining in the shouts of "*Vivent les Zouaves.*"

Eugénie and Clothilde watched from their carriage. Truth to tell, Eugénie was feeling more than a tinge of regret at relinquishing her Regentship. She had tasted power and had enjoyed it. From now on she was determined she would insist on being consulted on all national affairs.

★ ★ ★

The quiet, peaceful life of Biarritz was proving highly beneficial to the Emperor. No Walewskis to create discord; no monocled Plon-Plon leering down at her and criticising Lou-Lou's boisterous behaviour. Eugénie couldn't recall when life had been more harmonious.

It was when Prince Richard Metternich, together with his wife Pauline arrived at the Villa Eugénie, to present his credentials as the new Austrian Ambassador, that Court life took a new turn.

The Prince was young, good-looking, fond of women and Eugénie immediately found herself drawn by his gay, bawdy banter as a catalyst to her own prudish nature. As for his wife, when she was presented to Eugénie, Richard laughingly teased, "Ugly little monkey isn't she?"

It was true. Pauline Metternich could lay no claim to beauty, yet there was something fascinating about her appearance. While Eugénie sought a kindly remark, Pauline, quick as a flash, answered her husband "*I may look like a monkey, but I am the best dressed monkey in Europe.*"

Louis, who was present had laughed uproariously, insisting that the young people stay with them until the Court returned to Paris.

Eugénie's court had never been strict or pompous. Indeed many visiting royalty had deplored its laxity and free and easy manner and to this atmosphere, Pauline Metternich added even more zest.

Within a few days of her arrival, she was entertaining the company with her rendering, complete with actions, of all the latest bawdy songs being sung by the comediennes of Paris and Vienna.

Everyone applauded, even Paca, usually so quiet and retiring, turning to her Mother, Donna Manuelo, whispering, "This Princess Metternich could be the very friend 'Gena needs . . . someone to confide . . . someone to trust."

Donna Maneulo grunted, "If she doesn't become the Emperor's next mistress."

"I don't think so. She and her husband appear to be happily married . . . "

"Pooh. What woman wouldn't jump at the chance of being the Emperor's mistress? But, on second thoughts, perhaps that odd little face of hers might not suit His Majesty. He likes to have beautiful women around him. Granted Pauline Metternich is amusing, but . . . "

Eugénie and Pauline too, were having an aside conversation.

"Remember, Pauline what you said the day we met? Concerning your being the . . . the . . . "

"Best dressed monkey? Yes, I remember . . . "

"Each time you wear a different dress, I become more aware of the fact. Not about the monkey," she added laughingly, "but your dresses have something that mine lack. Who is your dressmaker?"

"Monsieur Worth of Paris. He is an Englishman . . ."

"So? As soon as we get back to the Tuileries, he must wait upon me. It would appear I have been missing the services of a creative genius."

★ ★ ★

Eugénie regarded the man standing before her with interest. Charles Frederick Worth. Faultlessly dressed; of impeccable manners, he made an immediate appeal to her impulsive nature, inviting him to be seated.

"Do I address you as Mons. Worth or Mr. Worth," she asked, amusement in her eyes, "for I understand you are an Englishman."

"That is so, Your Majesty, but I have now been in Paris for fourteen years, that I feel myself to be a Frenchman."

"What brought you to France in the

first place?" she asked curiously.

He shrugged his shoulders in the manner that only a Frenchman can, putting in a wealth of unspoken information.

"Ambition . . . desire to get out of a rut . . . "

"Were you a dressmaker in England?"

"Oh, no, Your Majesty, I worked as a counter-hand for Swan and Edgar in Piccadilly. I heard of your wonderful shops in Paris and decided to try my luck though I could not speak a word of French and arrived with but a hundred and seventeen francs in my pocket."

"Please go on. I find your story most intriguing."

"I was fortunate in obtaining a situation with Mons. Gagelin, the silk mercer in the Rue de Richelieu and still more fortunate to meet the most delightful shopgirl, who is now my wife."

"Now your story becomes romantic. But how did success come your way?"

"Handling rich silks, satins and velvets fascinated me. The manner in which they could be made to drape into soft folds; or be gathered into pleats, first set me dreaming and then actually creating a gown, using my wife as a model. When Mons. Gagelin saw my work, he immediately opened a dressmaking department putting me in charge."

"But how? Without any training or apprenticeship?"

"Perhaps on the practical side, Your Majesty, I should give some credit to my wife."

"Ah. I am glad to hear you say that. Wives can be of the most valuable assistance to their husbands. Perhaps it was she who persuaded you to leave Mons. Gagelin . . . ."

"Yes, Your Majesty. When foreign buyers came and admired my gowns, it was she who suggested I opened my own salon."

"Which is situated, where?"

"At 7 Rue de la Paix, Your Majesty."

"Princess Metternich tells me that you have your own unique way of designing a gown. Also that you have many new materials and new ideas for trimming."

"The Princess is most kind and flattering."

"I am giving a ball in April for the

opening of Hotel d'Alba, the mansion just completed for my sister, the Duchess of Alba. You shall make my gown for the occasion. You will be hearing from my secretary. Au revoir, Mons. Worth."

Charles Frederick Worth bowed himself out, knowing the house of Worth had reached its highest pinnacle.

Eugénie too, was pleased with her prospects. If Pauline was the best dressed monkey in Europe, she was going to be the best dressed woman!

The ball at Hotel d'Alba was to be fancy dress for those who chose, but M. Worth should make for her the most fantastic crinoline ever.

Dear, dear Paca. It would be wonderful to have her sister more or less resident in Paris. The Hotel d'Alba was to be the most magnificent mansion in the capital. No expense had been spared in its decoration or furnishing. It was a token of her love, not only for Paca but for James, Duke of Alba.

8

IT was the first Christmas they had spent without Paca and her family, but the Duke had written, his wife had been ill for several weeks, and the doctors were insisting on a quiet convalescence. Of course they had known of her malaise, but as Paca had always made light of it, they had fully expected her to be well enough to join them for the festivities. Eugénie was overwhelmed by depression while Lou-Lou wept bitterly when told his cousins would not be coming. The children made up a lively quartet; Lou-Lou, the youngest, but a very self-willed little boy, Carlos the eldest, exerting his advantage of the extra years in a gentle, amiable manner, while the two girls alternatively squabbled with and idolised their Imperial cousin.

Eugénie was an adoring aunt, chiefly because they were the children of Paca and James; the two people she loved more than anyone else, but also because by their childish caprices, they caused a breeze of reality to blow through the ostentatious, lavishly furnished palaces.

Indeed, she often thought, they were almost as dear to her as her own son. There was so much she wanted to do for them; Carlos must be given a position of eminence; the girls would move in the highest ranks of society; enabling them to make good marriages. Marquinita was already showing great promise of beauty, and dear little Chiquita with her piquant, elfish charm, would never lack for admirers.

That was why it was so important, that the Alba family should have strong roots in Paris, at the very heart of the French Empire. As soon as Paca was well enough to leave Madrid, they would be taking up residence in the Hotel d'Alba, in readiness for its inauguration ball in April.

★ ★ ★

It was the most wonderful masked ball that Paris could remember. Among the thousands of guests many had come from the farthest corners of Europe. Never before could they recall such a varied collection of fancy-dressed characters; never before had they enjoyed such food and wines brought from all parts of the world.

With Johann Strauss conducting his vast orchestra, the lilting music floated out on to the Champs d'Elysées, enabling the citizens to participate in the dancing.

M. Worth had created for Eugénie a crinoline of indescribable beauty, the vast skirt having a hundred and sixty-three lace-edged flounces, but she found no joy in its wearing, for after months of weary waiting Paca was still not well enough to leave Spain.

When Eugénie first learned of the doctors' decision, her immediate impulse was to cancel the event, but she was quick to realise the impossibility. How could she cancel those thousands of invitations and the vast catering preparations?

She was the Empress Eugénie of France, and as such, she must not show her innermost feelings. She was grateful that Louis had at last tired of Madame Walewska, for now their life was again more harmonious, so that with him by her side, and the staunch friendship of Pauline Metternich she was able to present the façade of a charming, gracious hostess, dancing first with one of her gentlemen and then another, as though she hadn't a care in the world.

It was July before the Albas arrived in Paris. Eugénie was shocked at her sister's fragile appearance, but Paca only laughed at her consternation.

"There's nothing to worry about 'Gena. Indeed the doctors cannot diagnose anything really wrong with me."

"Then why all these months in bed?"

"Ridiculous . . . save that I am everlastingly tired."

"Well now, I am sending my own doctors to see you. They are more advanced. They will soon have you well again."

Eugénie was more concerned than she liked to admit. Towards the end of August, she and Louis were to make a tour of Savoy, Nice and then on to Algeria. She put forward the suggestion that the tour might be postponed, but Paca scorned the idea.

"You will be away but three weeks . . . Here I am, surrounded by doctors, nurses, a household of servants, my husband . . . my mother . . . " She smiled whimsically. "Truthfully, 'Gena. I shall miss you, because it has been so long since we were together . . . "

Eugénie hugged her. "That's just how I feel. We must make the most of our time, before the tour begins."

Every evening she called on Paca. Often they would be seen driving down the Bois de Boulogne, the beautiful, elegant Empress; the gentle, fragile-looking duchess, but there came the evening when Eugénie came to say au-revoir.

"Thank goodness, and the French doctors that you are much improved. Otherwise I vow, the Emperor would have to go alone."

"The time will quickly pass, 'Gena."

"Yes, I will write every day; tell you of all the excitements. In the meantime, promise me, dear Paca, you will obey the doctors. They tell me, you are most stubborn and disobedient."

"You are becoming as fussy as Mama."

"But seriously, Paca, *mend your ways and endeavour to behave yourself while I am away.*"

The sisters embraced, tears in their eyes. Both were feeling the parting acutely, having only been together a few weeks.

"When we get back, we shall be going to Biarritz." Eugénie whispered. "There we shall be together all the time. Lazy days with the children; far more enjoyable than Algeria."

★ ★ ★

So far the tour had been most successful, being received everywhere with wild enthusiasm. Each day, in addition to sending a telegram to Paca, she found time to write a long letter, endeavouring in doing so, to ease her own anxiety.

They had reached Marseilles, where that night they were to be entertained at a ball, the guests numbering 150,000. As they were due to sail for Algeria the next morning, she wrote,

'Adieu, my dear sister. I do not know whether I shall be able to write again before we return from Algiers, but you may be sure that if I don't, it will be through lack of time, and not from laziness, for you know that I love you tenderly.'

After a weekend on board *L'Aigle*, they reached Algiers on Monday, where, to Eugénie's great distress, a telegram awaited them reporting a relapse in Paca's condition.

Immediately Eugénie telegraphed the Duke, asking for more news by return. All that day, as they drove from one reception to another, cheered by hordes of dusky natives, Eugénie was in torment.

"Could we not curtail the tour, and return home now?" she pleaded with Louis.

He shook his head. "All the important chiefs in North Africa are gathered here to entertain us tomorrow night. If we were to leave now, they would regard it as an insult. Courage, Eugénie, courage."

They spent the next day relaxing in preparation for the night's entertainment, but Eugénie could not rest, waiting and hoping for a re-assuring telegram.

When Louis came to her room, to take her down to their waiting carriage, he held his breath in wonderment. Never had Eugénie looked so regal; so resplendent. M. Worth had excelled himself. The bunches of flowers that embellished her many-tiered crinoline, were each centred by jewels; rubies or emeralds, and the belt at her waist was encrusted with the same flashing gems. A tiara of diamonds, scintillated atop her red-curls and her accentuated eyebrows were more marked than usual . . . a truly entrancing and compelling figure.

He could not withhold his admiration. "Chérie . . . Chérie. You are magnificent . . . so very beautiful . . ."

She interrupted brusquely. "Louis. Has any more news come through?"

For a moment he hesitated, then impatiently, "No. No."

Picking up her fan, she murmured hopefully, "They do say, no news is good news."

★ ★ ★

Eugénie had not known what to expect at this reception, but when the Beys and Chieftains, some completely robed in dazzling white; others arrayed in brilliant colours, all prostrated themselves before her, their swarthy faces alight with admiration, a feeling of elation and delight enveloped her, almost to a point of recklessness. Many of them spoke French, and she found herself in animated conversation, accepting cigarette after cigarette, and dancing into the early morning. For a few brief hours, she had been able to forget.

It was when Pepa was preparing her for bed, that Louis came to her room. There had been a telegram.

"Tell me quickly. How is she?"

"No improvement."

"Oh God! Oh God! Louis . . . we must return."

"Yes. I will make our apologies. We shall be cutting the tour by only two days. I will give orders *L'Aigle* be ready to put out to sea with the next tide."

Her voice was almost humble. "Thank you, Louis. Thank you. Pray God, we are not too late."

★ ★ ★

L'Aigle made Marseilles in record time and the royal train was waiting, Eugénie impatiently begrudging every moment spent in thanking officials for their speedy preparations.

She was glad of the privacy of her salon on the train, but hardly had it pulled out, before she was joined by Louis.

For a moment, he did not speak, then "Eugénie, ma chérie you must be very brave . . . "

She sat up, gripping the arms of the chair, staring him full in the face. "What are you telling me?"

He dropped to his knees beside her, taking her hands in his. "Paca is dead," he said gently.

She drew in a long breath, then began to sob loudly. He did not attempt to either restrain or comfort her, rising to take a chair by the window, watching the landscape sliding away.

At last the sobbing ceased, and in a broken voice she asked. "When . . . when did it happen?"

His answer was slow in coming. "Last Sunday."

"Last Sunday? But today is Friday! Surely . . . surely, we could have had news before now." There was incredulity in her voice.

Again the hesitation. "I received the news on Tuesday . . . "

"On Tuesday? The day of the reception? You actually knew as we drove along . . . you knew as . . . "

Her voice was taking on the well-known dreaded high-pitched anger.

"I could not tell you Eugénie. You would have been in no fit state to receive the Algerian chieftains."

"That telegram was meant for me. You preferred that I should go, eating and drinking, and making merry, while my sister lay dead. As in the Plombières affair, you could not trust me to rise above my grief. How little you know me! I could have been the Empress of France for a few brief hours, before succumbing to my sisterly love."

"Perhaps I did misjudge you Eugénie," he mumbled.

" . . . and why could you not have told

160

me that same night, or on board *L'Aigle* crossing from Algiers? Why wait until now?" Pausing only to take breath, the inexorable, scornful voice went on, "Shall I tell you why? Because you are a coward . . . a moral coward . . . you are weak-willed. You cannot make decisions . . . " Her flow of words came to an abrupt halt, joining Louis in gazing out of the window, before resuming in a calmer voice, "Is there any other information?"

Without turning, he answered dully, "The funeral service took place yesterday . . . "

Eugénie let out a shriek of mixed anger and grief, " . . . and I wasn't there to take my last farewell . . . "

"Be reasonable, Eugénie. Had we cancelled the reception and made an immediate turnabout, we should only have arrived in Paris yesterday . . . "

"Yes, but in time for the funeral." The sobbing began again.

Louis' voice was abject. "I have telegraphed the Duke to wait until you return, before . . . before he takes . . . " His voice trailed into silence.

" . . . Paca's body back to Spain. Go on! Say it! Why do the words stick in

161

your throat? We should never have gone on this tour. I should never have left her . . . "

★ ★ ★

In the hall of St. Cloud, James, Duke of Alba, dressed in sombre black, stood waiting. Eugénie took one glance at him and then running, threw herself into his arms, murmuring between her sobs, "Oh, Jimmy . . . Jimmy . . . "

Gentle, he led her to a sofa and let her weep, until he became aware she was whispering, "Tell me everything."

"There is little to tell 'Gena. There was this relapse, but no worse than on other occasions. In a couple of days, she was well again, laughing and joking. Indeed she was laughing only five minutes before she died."

"Were you there?"

"No, only her maid."

"How terrible . . . that she was alone . . . none of her loved ones . . . "

"No 'Gena, it was not terrible. She died happy."

"But what of those of us who are

left?" She wailed.

"*To think that I was not there, near her, doubles my grief.*"

"Our loss is terrible yes, but . . ."

"Where . . . where . . . ?"

"Her coffin is still resting at the Madeleine, where the service was held yesterday."

"You will be taking it back to Spain."

"When certain formalities have been complied with."

"The children? Where are they?"

"The girls returned to Spain yesterday with Donna Manuelo."

Eugénie groaned. "She is no fit person to have charge of two young children. Her ways are too old fashioned. And what of Carlos?"

"I have kept him here in Paris. I had need of someone."

"Of course, dear Jimmy. Would you, oh would you please allow him to remain here? I would engage a tutor."

"There are many matters to be arranged."

"And Marquinita and Chiquita. Could I not have them in my care . . . my sister's children?"

"There are other matters to settle first."

"Of course. Of course. But in the meantime, you and Carlos must stay here at St. Cloud with me."

"That, I shall be only too happy to do. I cannot face living in that huge mansion. It has no happy memories of Paca . . . though I do thank you for your generosity."

"I understand, Jimmy, I understand. It shall be pulled down, brick by brick. I too, hate the place. I never want to cross its threshold again . . . "

★ ★ ★

Each day she visited the Madeleine to pray over Paca's coffin, continuing to do so, when Louis had it removed to the Malmaison Church at Rueil where his grandmother the Empress Josephine and his mother Queen Hortense were interred, but she could find no ease for her grief.

She and the Emperor were hardly on speaking terms and the Duke of Alba, with whom she shared the grief, had been compelled to return to Spain on business matters and to make arrangements for Paca's interment.

Finally, her nerves almost at breaking point she wrote him,

'Your house in Madrid, sad though it may be, at least reminds you of her life, but her house here brings back only the memory of the last few days and her death. I feel a voyage would do me good, for always being reminded of my loss, weakens me, but where can I go? I want to flee and I don't know where. Write to me dear Jimmy . . . '

She didn't wait for his advice, suddenly announcing to Louis, that she was going away for an indefinite period of time . . .

"But Eugénie, where are you going, without any arrangements? What will the nation think and say?"

She shrugged her shoulders, "I care not what they say. Perhaps," she went on with a malicious laugh, "they'll say I've left you. That I am tired of your amorous affairs and that I am seeking a divorce. Or more to the point, that your cruelty, in keeping back the news of my sister's death, has sent me out of my mind."

"Eugénie," he pleaded, "cannot you be more understanding . . . more forgiving . . . ?"

"At the moment, I understand but one thing, my sister is dead."

"And you think you will find comfort for your grief away from France? Where do you intend going?"

"I have a fancy to visit Scotland . . . "

"Scotland! At this time of the year? November?"

"You forget that my grandfather was a Scotsman . . . William Kirkpatrick . . . immigrant wine-merchant. I am not ashamed of my plebian ancestry. Perhaps that is why I feel the urge to visit Scotland."

"You . . . will you be visiting Her Majesty?"

"I have not decided. I shall write her that I am travelling incognito. I want peace . . . peace . . . "

★ ★ ★

166

She left Paris three days later, taking with her only one lady-in-waiting, her maid and a footman.

She had no fixed plans as to how long she was going to stay in London, but a suite of rooms had been secured for her at Claridge's Hotel.

With this scant information, Louis had to be content, and in an effort to suppress false rumours he issued the statement, *'Owing to the effect on Her Majesty of the death of her sister, the doctors have recommended a change of air. The Empress will visit Scotland in the strictest incognito.'*

It was a few days later when in conversation with Pauline Metternich, that he came nearer the truth.

"'Tis to be hoped sir, that her Majesty find satisfaction in Scotland, then I am sure her spirits will revive more quickly."

He looked puzzled, "What magic spell does Scotland possess to charm away grief . . . and unsatisfactory husbands?"

Now it was Pauline's face that was clouded with bewilderment, "But surely, sir, you know Her Majesty's main reason for going to Edinburgh?"

"No, I do not. I am completely in the dark. Pray enlighten me."

Her bewilderment gave place to dismay. "I am sorry, sir. It would appear, I have spoken out of place, the Empress not having confided in you."

"What is this she has told you? I demand to know. That is a command, Pauline."

She gave a sigh of resignation. "Her Majesty is deeply concerned about her own health . . . "

"Is Her Majesty ill?" The interruption was edged with fear.

"Not that she is aware . . . that is what pesters her. As you know sir, the doctors were never able to diagnose the real disease that the Duchess of Alba suffered, but it was in some way connected with the spine . . . "

She hesitated before going on, "Her Majesty at times suffers from the backache. It preys on her mind that she might be struck with the same complaint."

" . . . And she has gone to Edinburgh to find out? Are there no eminent doctors in Paris?"

"She is adamant, that nowhere in the

world are there such good doctors as in Scotland . . . "

He ignored her chatter. "You, I would say are more in Her Majesty's company than anyone. Do you think she is ill . . . in any danger?"

Pauline's little pug-like face gazed into that of Louis, "No, sir, I do not. We all have our share of aches and pains. Her Majesty's are no worse than those of her subjects . . . "

"Then why . . . ?"

"She is weighed down by grief . . . imagination. I am convinced, sir, all will be well, when she returns."

★ ★ ★

She had been away from France for a month, four whole weeks of constant endeavours to come to an understanding with her grief and anger over Louis' duplicity.

On her return to London, she had written Victoria, who had promptly invited her to Windsor, and here she was sitting by the side of Prince Albert, driving up to the castle. Her first impression at their meeting was that he appeared more stern and morose than ever, but stealing another glance at him, she was shocked to see how ill and tired he looked. Conversation between them was little more than polite enquiries, and she was glad when they arrived, as much as to escape his icy company as that of the bitterly cold December day.

Victoria's welcome more than made up for Albert's reticence; warm and effusive, full of sympathy, but lunch was a stiff formal meal with barely any conversation, until dessert, when the younger children joined them.

Eugénie was charmed with three-year-old Beatrice, and delighted to see Albert begin to thaw, as his small fair haired daughter clambered onto his knee after she had made a pretty little curtsy to the visitor.

Victoria however soon tired of the children, and as she and Eugénie retired to her drawing-room, the little royals went back to their nursery.

"They are so lovable when they are small, but as they grow older . . . " Victoria made a gesture of resignation.

"And now tell me what really brought you to England, and sent you all the way up to Scotland."

Eugénie spoke quietly. "I wished to see a reputable doctor, who, treating me incognito, could give me a straightforward assessment of my health."

"And have you received satisfaction?"

"Perfect satisfaction, I now feel assured I have no threatening disease hanging over me."

"I am glad to hear that. Certain other most alarming rumours were reaching us. Tell me Eugénie, just what did happen between you and Louis on that Algerian trip?"

Although taken aback by the bluntness of the question, Eugénie found herself telling Victoria the whole story.

The Queen's lips tightened. "It was most unforgivable of him." She paused, and then went on, "You will know we have recently returned from a visit to Germany."

"Indeed, yes. I was about to enquire about dear Vicky."

"Poor child. She has just given birth to another baby . . . a daughter . . . "

"But that is enchanting! A son . . . now a daughter!"

Victoria frowned. "Too soon. Too soon to have a second child. I warned her, but then we poor creatures are born for men's pleasure and amusement."

Eugénie could not meet Victoria's eyes. She had never made herself available for any man's pleasure, and as she made no enlargement on the subject, the Queen went on, "*It is in all clever men's nature. Dear Albert is not quite exempt*," she giggled "though he would not admit it."

"The little Prince William?" Eugénie interposed quickly, "Did you see him?"

"Oh yes, a fine little boy, save for his poor withered arm, but the doctors say it will be all right in time." She sighed. " . . . but Bertie is causing us more worry than ever. I daren't tell you of some of his escapades."

"We heard that marriage negotiations were being put forward on his behalf."

"All of which are likely to come to naught," she fumed. "He shows all the tendencies of taking after my wicked Hanoverian uncles. Women. Actress women . . . and tobacco!"

Eugénie gave a gentle laugh. "But that is part of a young man's education is it not?"

The Queen bridled, "Part of a young Frenchman's education, perhaps, but not that of the future King of England. His behaviour has caused Prince Albert and me great distress."

"I am sorry." She hesitated. "I thought the Prince did not look too well."

"He is very susceptible to the cold and stomach disorders . . . especially since his recent accident . . . "

"Accident?"

"He was driving a four in hand, when the horses bolted, and collided with a stationary wagon, throwing dear Albert into the roadway. He was terribly bruised and cut. It was a wonder he wasn't killed."

"Providence was looking after him, dear Victoria."

The Queen nodded. "Yes. God alone knows what I or England would do without him."

She was still in no mood to return to France but when she heard Paca's remains were being taken to Spain the following week, she was all haste.

The royal carriage was waiting for her at Boulogne and to her great surprise, Louis was there to meet her.

As he took her in his arms, she found herself responding with more pleasure than she had thought would ever be possible again. Like all travellers, she found it good to be home, but with the renewal of the daily visits to weep and pray over Paca's coffin, the grief returned as heavy as before.

Louis watched with mounting concern but Pauline was quick to reassure him. "The sooner the remains of the Duchess are removed the sooner will the Empress regain her high spirits, particularly now she has no qualms about her health."

It was just a week before Christmas, that Paca's journey home to Spain began; Eugénie distraught and pitiful in her grief but everyone else giving a sigh of relief, wondering just what kind of a Christmas Her Majesty was going to allow the Court.

9

EUGÉNIE beamed with pleasure as James Alba presented the young man he had brought along to the Villa Eugénie.

"Senor José Hidalgo, Your Majesty."

The man bowed low. She was quick to note the elegance of his bearing and clothes and when he lifted his face, she was charmed by his smiling good looks.

"You are most welcome, Senor Hidalgo. Come, sit down and tell me of yourself."

"I am in the Mexican diplomatic service . . . "

"Mexico! Ah, affairs are in a sorry state there."

"You are interested in my country, Your Majesty?"

"Of a certainty. France has sent several thousand soldiers and a vast amount of money to help oust Benito Juarez. Naturally we are interested. We wish to see the return of our money which he is withholding."

Senor Hidalgo sighed. "I see no prospect of that, Your Majesty until there is a settled regime. Mexico needs a monarch. An Emperor to rule supreme . . . "

She laughed. "I do believe you have been sent to Europe to find yourself a monarch . . . an army . . . and money."

"You are very discerning, Your Majesty or am I so very naïve?"

"No. You interest me. I will speak to the Emperor."

For the rest of the day and evening, she went about in a state of self absorption. Senor Hidalgo had set in motion a burning ambition, that France, urged by the Empress, should play the leading role in the foundation of a Mexican monarchy.

She could not sleep. Sitting by the window of her boudoir she stared over the sea, the moon spilling on the waves as they broke on the beach and rocks.

Then she saw him. He too, was sitting in his castle, high up the cliffs, watching the sea, as restless as his frustrated mind; yearning for active occupation. The Archduke Maximilian of Austria in his castle at Miramar. The very man . . . a Habsburg . . . reared in royal pomp and splendour.

★ ★ ★

The December afternoon was closing in, the dusk being hastened by the swirling fog giving the company of riders, horses and hounds a phantom-like appearance only belied by the gay chatter and the baying of the hounds.

At the head of the party, rode Eugénie and Senor Hidalgo together with several other Mexican guests she had invited to Compiègne. Reaching the courtyard of the Palace, she asked, "Have you enjoyed the hunt, gentlemen?"

"Si, si, Your Majesty. A perfect day's sport."

She dismounted, giving the reins to a waiting groom, "Then I will see you at dinner," and walked up the wide stone steps wondering as to how she would find Louis, who that morning had been prostrated by pain, totally unable to ride.

To her surprise he was waiting in the

great hall, impatiently walking up and down.

"Ah, there you are, chérie. Please . . . please come into my study."

"But why? My habit is saturated and muddy . . . "

"It is important. A telegram from England . . . "

"From England?" She almost snatched the proffered paper.

She had to read the stilted message three or four times before she could convince herself she had read aright.

Prince Albert was dead. But how? Why? He was a young man. Then her thoughts flew to Victoria. Poor dear Victoria. She would be distraught and crazy with grief.

Louis' voice broke in. "I have sent a telegram expressing our grief and condolences."

"Thank you. I must write to Victoria immediately."

When Pepa would have removed her riding-boots, she waved her away, sitting huddled up in the bedraggled green riding-habit.

The news from England was dismal. Although it was now more than six months since the death of Albert, Victoria had gone into seclusion at Osborne, refusing to attend all Privy Councils. Rumours had begun to reach Paris, she was placing the onus of the Prince's death upon Edward, Prince of Wales. Just when negotiations concerning his betrothal to Alexandra of Denmark were making favourable progress, news had broken of his affair with an actress. Albert had lost no time in travelling to Cambridge to chastise his erring son. He had caught cold on the journey, the beginning of the end. Victoria would never forgive Bertie.

The Mexican project was progressing with frustrating tardiness. Maximilian was interested, but cautious. His duchess, Carlotta, however was the dominant personality and was gradually wearing down the Archduke's doubts.

★ ★ ★

Despite Edward's affair with the actress, Princess Alexandra and her family were prepared to forgive and in March, 1863, the marriage took place at Windsor, the Queen still insisting on wearing mourning and watching the service from a gallery.

Eugénie was glad for Edward. No longer would he be ruled by elderly tutors chosen by his mother. No longer would she be able to dictate his comings and goings. She had already invited him to bring his bride to Paris.

She wished the Mexican venture would move with a little more rapidity. She was becoming restive and fidgety. More and more troops had been sent out. Surely it was time Maximilian made his bid for the throne. She found herself losing patience over trivialities; hasty and quick tempered with her ladies. Perhaps that was why she always felt a nagging irritation whenever she met a certain woman driving through the park at St. Cloud; a woman who had never been presented at Court. Yet whenever Louis accompanied her on the drive and they met this person, he was always quick to doff his hat and be rewarded by a radiant smile. Who was she? She was too proud to enquire of Louis, lest the creature be one of his many 'sisters of joy' who he regularly visited. Yet she didn't look like a prostitute. She was young with moderate good looks.

Her annoyance, however, changed to outraged dignity, when, their carriages meeting almost head-on, she saw the odious creature kissing her finger-tips to the beaming Louis. A torrent of angry questions rose in her mind, but recalling the two footmen standing behind her open carriage, she managed to control her temper. Yet on arriving back at the palace, she found she could not confront him. It was as though she already knew and wished to put off the moment of truth.

In her dejection, she turned to Pauline Metternich. "I beg of you . . . find out who she is . . . where she lives . . . "

Pauline's findings were shattering. When Eugénie noticed her hesitancy, she demanded sharply, "What is the mystery? I demand to be told."

"She is a certain Mlle Marguerite Bellanger . . . "

"Go on . . . "

"She lives in the Villa . . . the first villa adjoining the royal park."

"And what else did you learn?"

Pauline drew in a long breath, "You really want to know, Your Majesty?"

"Perhaps I myself can supply the answer. The Emperor is a regular visitor."

A silence fell between them. Pauline was the first to speak. "Do not concern yourself too much, Madame. It could be a fleeting affair. There is no possibility of her becoming a maîtresse de titre . . . she lacks breeding. The Emperor would never bring her to Court."

Eugénie refused to be comforted, her anger increasing daily. Since the dismissal of Madame Walewska almost three years ago, they had lived in comparative amicability. Oh, there had been the cheap tawdry assignations, which had bothered her not one jot, but that he should install a woman in a house almost adjoining the Palace, it was not to be borne.

After a succession of refusals to join him in an afternoon drive, and knowing

182

the Court was talking, Louis went up to her sitting-room to ascertain the truth of her trivial excuses.

She stared at him coldly. "I would have thought, you preferred to meet your mistress, Mlle Bellanger, without having your wife by your side . . . "

Shrugging his shoulders he smiled broadly showing no confusion, "Ah, Mlle. Bellanger. Yes, she is a dear friend."

"Friend? Whore! Scum! And you dare bring her to St. Cloud."

"I prefer that she lives near. It makes my coming and going so much more simple . . . "

"You dare to stand there and openly admit . . . ?" There was screaming rage in her voice.

"What would you have me do? Deny it? I am not ashamed of the relationship."

"*Sacre bleu!* Next you will be telling me you are in love with her."

"Exactly. I am in love with her. She is gentle and loving . . . "

"Spare me the sentimental details. You fool, cannot you see, any woman can be loving and gentle if it gives her the doubtful honour of being the Emperor's mistress."

"I have already asked Mlle. Bellanger not to drive in the Park at your customary time . . . "

"I care not what she does . . . nor for that matter what you do, but let me advise you of your infrequency at Council meetings. Perhaps they already know that you prefer the arms of your mistress . . . "

"You wrong me Eugénie. You know that I am frequently indisposed . . . in great pain . . . often heavily sedated . . . "

"All the more reason then you should not visit this . . . this . . . "

"I go to her for quiet relaxation away from all talk of internal politics; the everlasting problem of Mexico; for soothing comfort when I am in pain . . . "

"It is a doctor you need . . . not a mistress. What can she do for you?"

He sighed, turning to leave the room. "You would not understand, Eugénie. You would not understand."

Paris in the Spring of 1864, seemed to Eugénie, more beautiful than ever. It was not so much the profusion of scented flowers nor the ostentatious street decorations in honour of the visit of Archduke Maximilian and his Duchess, Carlotta, but the satisfaction that her dream was about to come true.

Next month, her guests would be setting sail for Mexico, having taken the Imperial oath, accepting the crown.

When the time came to say farewell, Eugénie and Carlotta were in high spirits but the two emperors were in a much more sober mood. There were affectionate embraces as a military band played first the newly composed Mexican national anthem, then the Austrian and finally 'Partant Pour La Syrie'. Then they were in the carriage, driving away with an escort of Cent-Gardes and the full-throated cheers of Paris citizens.

Eugénie, bubbling with excitement turned to Louis. "Just imagine! In a few months' time, they will be driving through their own capital, with their own escort . . . "

"I do not envy Maximilian. I would never have blamed him if he had refused the crown."

She gave him a look of contempt. "You

are devoid of all courage and resolve. Maximilian is little better; everlastingly wavering and changing his mind. Thank God, Carlotta is made of stronger metal."

10

WITHIN the month, Eugénie was again entertaining royal visitors, none other than the Prince and Princess of Wales. Edward was in very high spirits. "Only married a year," he boasted, "and already London society is coming to life again. Our London residence is ideal for entertaining on a large scale, while Sandringham, our country house is a veritable hide-away for house-parties and high jinks."

Eugénie's voice was inviting. "How would you like to sample some of our high jinks? A Parisian music-hall?"

Edward's eyes sparkled. "Indeed, yes . . . " but Louis hurriedly interposed, "Would that be wise in view of Her Majesty's . . . er . . . outlook . . . ?"

"Meaning that she considers Paris another Sodom and Gomorrah?"

"Why not, sir?" There was a coaxing plea in the Prince's voice.

Louis' reply was an expressive shrug,

"As you will then."

Eugénie was now as animated as her guests. "Where shall we go? I know. The Alcazar . . . to hear Thérèsa."

"Are not her songs a little too . . . too risqué for . . . "

"They are not children. It is settled." She turned to Alexandra. "We will dress simply. Inconspicuously. Thérèsa is the rage of Paris. You will enjoy the show." Thérèsa was all Eugénie had promised. Whether Alexandra and Edward had sufficient command of the French language to understand the double meanings of her songs, Eugénie did not know, but they were laughing hilariously at her miming and gestures which were distinctly vulgar, yet not without a certain fascination.

The applause was deafening and it was only after several encores that Thérèsa was able to make a final exit.

Glancing through his programme, Louis remarked, "Nothing else of any merit. Shall we . . . ?"

"Go elsewhere? Most certainly. The night is still young." Eugénie rose and taking Edward's arms went out to their waiting carriage, instructing the coachman, 'La Closerie des Lilas.'

It was a comparatively small theatre and to aid their incognito they took a box, where they could sit well back from the public gaze.

For a while they watched several acts and listened to more bawdy songs but with such a difference from Thérèsa's that they were distinctly boring.

It wasn't until, introduced by loud pulsating music, a line of dancing girls came on stage, arms interlocked behind them, performing a series of high-kicks, displaying a tantalising froth of lace petticoats.

Their costumes were lavish and glamorous, décolletée, but not indecently so; the bodices were heavily sequined and the satin skirts long and full. In their hair they wore huge feathers which bobbed and dipped as they danced.

Eugénie smiled as both Edward and Louis moved to the front of the box. The girls had now unlocked arms and to the accompaniment of shrieks and yells were holding their skirts and petticoats up to their shoulders, still kicking high giving a provocative display of black suspenders, bare thighs and frilly lace drawers.

There were whistles of delight from the audience as the music grew still louder and the pace quickened. Now the bevy of beauty had turned its back to the footlights but there was no slackening in their athletic prowess. Then, unexpectedly, with an ear-splitting whoop, the skirts were audaciously lifted over their heads, giving an even more daring display of their frivolous underwear.

There were movements in the audience as men tried to get out of their seats to reach the stage, but attendants were quick to deal with them.

Once again the routine was resumed with the precision of Cent-Gardes, but suddenly the leader of the line, stepped forward and effortlessly performed a cartwheel . . . then the next dancer until the stage was a whirling mass of legs and lace.

The auditorium rocked with applause but still beaming, the girls were back in line, still kicking, still displaying flesh and frills, still giving voice to whoops and shouts until the theatre was full of a demoniacal cacophany of blaring music and female stridency.

Then, piercing the pandemonium, came a succession of blood-curdling yells, as first one girl and then another jumped high in the air, to come down on the boards in a 'split' till the whole line of nodding plumes were raised to reveal the smiling but perspiring faces of the dancers.

No-one was more generous with applause than Edward. As they drove back to The Tuileries, the Can-Can dance was his sole topic of conversation. What girls! What gorgeous creatures! Noting the excited, venal gleam in his eyes, so familiar in Louis, when a pretty woman hove in sight, Eugénie felt a stab of fear for Alexandra's future happiness.

★ ★ ★

Letters from Carlotta had begun to reach France. All was well. They had been accepted as Emperor and Empress of Mexico which was a truly beautiful country. Thank God, Eugénie sighed.

If only her own affairs were not in such a sorry state.

Marguerite Bellanger had given birth to a child; Louis' child. How could he so degrade himself? He must be the laughing-stock of every salon . . . every wine-shop, but Louis seemed oblivious of any criticism; all his spare time being spent with Marguerite.

"It won't last, Ma'am," comforted Pauline Metternich, but Eugénie sensed this was no shallow affair. Never had she so longed for the time to pass before they were due to go to Biarritz but when the weeks came and went without Louis arranging their departure, she was finally compelled to raise the question.

He had the grace to appear somewhat embarrassed. "I am glad you have spoken of it. I shall not be going to Biarritz this year."

"Not going? But why? Surely you are not staying in Paris?"

"No. I have decided to take a rest in Vichy."

She stared at him as though she did not understand, then slowly the truth dawned. "You are going with that . . . that . . . woman . . . "

"Yes. I am going with Mlle. Bellanger."

"But why, Louis, why? Am I not more important . . . your wife . . . and Lou-Lou . . . your son?"

He passed a hand wearily over his eyes. "I need a rest. I am often in such low health . . . "

"But you would find rest at Biarritz . . . "

"No, it would not be the same. I want to be away from everyone."

"Except Mlle. Bellanger . . . "

"Yes, except Mlle. Bellanger. You see, Eugénie . . . you see . . . she loves me . . . she gives me the comfort I so badly need . . . "

"You talk like a lovesick fool." There was contempt in every word. "And I suppose you think you are in love with her?"

"I don't know. What is love, Eugénie? I loved you wholeheartedly but I found no response in you."

"Whereas Mlle Bellanger makes willing response . . . with her body. Go with her then. Go where you will. Let the whole French nation know of your whoredom . . . "

193

★ ★ ★

She could not stay in Paris to bear the brunt of all the gossip, so assuming the title of Comtesse de Pierrefonds, she went to Schwalbach, a watering-place in Hesse-Nassau, taking with her only three of her ladies.

There, in the midst of beautiful, peaceful surroundings, her volatile spirits quickly rose, so great her peace of mind, that she lingered into the middle of October before returning to Paris.

Louis greeted her with courtesy and friendliness. It was indeed good to be back but her new-found tranquillity was swiftly shattered when she learned Louis was living at the villa.

She sought the advice of Prosper Merimee.

"What can I do to bring him to his senses . . . back to his duty to France?" she asked frantically.

He regarded her with compassion. "At the moment there is nothing you can do. You must wait until the affair dies its natural death . . . as it will do . . . as all the others have done."

"But how long must I endure this humiliation? I hear that he is passionately fond of the child."

"The Emperor has always had a great tenderness for children . . ."

"But this child binds him to her . . . keeps him enslaved . . . " She paced the floor in agitation, "I cannot tolerate this odious situation much longer."

★ ★ ★

There were often days, when Louis did not attend the daily meeting with his ministers, sending a note that he was too ill to be present. Then it was that Eugénie, had to stand in for him, even to the signing of documents. Now with his attendance so sporadic, she put in an appearance at every meeting, so as to be informed of all political developments. Someday, perhaps not too far away, Louis' ill-health would compel him to abdicate in favour of his young son, and she would be Empress Regent until his coming of age. It would be the zenith of her ambition.

Yet she recoiled in dismay and shock,

when entering his study one morning, she found him sprawled across his desk, unconscious.

Quickly she rang for aid, but before the doctor arrived, Louis opened his eyes, murmuring, "It is nothing . . . only the pain."

He was still wearing the clothes he had worn yesterday afternoon. He had not dined at the Palace, and had obviously spent the night at the Villa. A wave of savage fury overwhelmed her. All very well to scoff and deride her for her prudish outlook on sensual behaviour, but this constant indulgence on Louis' part was beyond all understanding. Marguerite Bellanger was a young woman, but Louis was not a young man!

With the doctors in attendance, she lost no time. The moment of action had arrived. She would face this vile woman, and seeking someone to accompany her, ordered her carriage.

Her choice of companion fell on Mons. Mocquard, brother of the Emperor's secretary. When he heard of their venue and the nature of the visit, which Eugénie explained with excited volubility, the poor man endeavoured to excuse himself.

"I do not think the Emperor would wish me to be present . . . "

"I do not intend that you shall participate in the conversation. I merely require you to accompany me as a formal necessity."

Marguerite Bellanger rose and curtsied as Eugénie entered her drawing-room. She was a tall, fair girl in her middle twenties, strong and healthy looking, a puzzled frown clouding her face as she waited for the Empress to speak.

"I presume the Emperor stayed here last night . . . "

"He did, Your Majesty," came the quiet reply.

"And you sent him back to the Palace this morning, in a state of collapse after last night's orgy."

"There was no orgy, Your Majesty."

"Then how do you account for his deplorable state?"

"His Majesty is a sick man . . . "

"Then knowing that, why do you encourage him? *You are killing him.* You must give him up. Tell him he must visit you no more."

Mons. Mocquard waiting in the hall could hear Eugénie's voice raised in anger. "What he sees in you, I cannot tell. You have no birth, no breeding, no intelligence, mother of a bastard . . . "

Now Marguerite was losing her temper. "What right have you to come here and insult me?"

"The right to demand, you relinquish all claims on the Emperor. Oh, he will see to it that you are made financially secure. He is considerate in that way, to all his mistresses, but I insist that he ceases to visit you."

"Why do you think he comes here — " Eugénie's answer was a contemptuous low laugh. "As if we didn't both know."

"So you know that you bore him? Pester him with ridiculous trivialities? Attack him with your violent temper?"

"How dare you?"

"How dare I? Because he comes here for relaxation. To sit by my fire . . . to doze while I play and sing to him. To comfort him when he is in pain. If you don't wish the Emperor to come here, why do you not concern yourself more with his well-being?"

Eugénie found herself lost for words. This woman was actually in love with Louis.

"Listen, Mam'selle. Your association with the Emperor is causing considerable scandal." She sighed wearily. "I am accustomed to these affairs but it is bad for the Empire; that the Emperor's behaviour should be so scurrilously discussed by the gutter-press. Suppose he was to die in your house? The throne would become so insecure for my son . . . "

Whether it was the mention of death or the allusion to the Prince but Eugénie found she could no longer restrain her emotion. Then, to her amazement, Marguerite, too, was weeping.

For a few moments there was silence in the room as both women composed themselves and dried away their tears. Then Eugénie rose.

"I must return and speak with the doctors as to the Emperor's condition . . . "

" . . . and I, Your Majesty, will move out of the Villa . . . away from St. Cloud. I will write the Emperor."

Eugénie smiled. "Thank you for being

so understanding . . . and so good to my husband."

As the door opened, Mons. Mocquard beheld the amazing sight of Eugénie embracing Marguerite.

11

ON the doctor's advice, Louis had again gone to Vichy, but this time, alone, leaving Eugénie to attend to all ministerial affairs. Although enjoying the powers invested in her, she had for some time, felt depressed concerning the constant demands of Maximilian for more money and troops. Each time, they had replied they could send no more money and the time had come for the recall of the troops. What could have gone wrong in Mexico?

She looked up from the document she was studying as Mons. Mocquard was admitted. "A telegram, Your Majesty. I thought you should have it without delay."

A telegram! Louis ill? Worse? As she read, agitation and bewilderment showed in her face. "It is from Carlotta! Empress of Mexico! She is here in France! Coming to Paris! What am I to do?"

"The Emperor must be informed. He must return."

"Yes! Yes! Immediately."

Within a few hours of the message being sent, another telegram arrived. Carlotta was already in the Capital! Eugénie acted swiftly, arranging to call on her the next day. But what was she going to say? How was she going to deal with her demands?

★ ★ ★

It was while Eugénie was with Carlotta, that Louis arrived back at St. Cloud and impatiently awaited to hear what had passed between them.

"She insists upon seeing you," she told him bluntly.

Louis groaned. "I will not see her. I cannot see her. I am so truly sorry for her and Maximilian . . . and to have to refuse . . . no, I will not see her."

She sighed impatiently. "Unless you meet her when she arrives, she threatens to storm your bedroom."

"But what can I say to her?"

"You must be firm . . . no matter how

202

much she weeps."

"Poor, poor Carlotta."

"You are too sentimental . . . too soft-hearted. A pretty woman and you are lost but this time you have not to think of Carlotta as a woman but as a country . . . Mexico, and yourself, not as a besotted man, but of France. Which Empire do you wish to survive? Mexico or France?"

As he made no answer, she went on remorselessly, "You will see her and you will tell her, no more money, no more men."

When Carlotta arrived, there were polite kisses and greetings but Eugénie, as quickly as possible led the way to Louis' study.

Without waiting to be seated, Carlotta turned to Louis. "Here is a letter from the Emperor of Mexico, stating the sorry plight of his country . . . "

"Pray do be seated, dear Carlotta . . . " With shuffling gait, Louis led her to a chair, glad to sink his own aching body into another, nearby.

"I think General Almonte, who you sent over some months ago, has explained . . . "

"I do not want explanations from either General Almonte . . . or you . . . I want action."

"But you must realise, I alone can do nothing. I must consult my ministers. It is they who are insisting on the recall of French troops . . . "

"But just another year . . . "

"No, dear Empress, *the time has come when you must cease indulging in illusions.* Until the last few months, you have written of your successful government; painted pictures of a rich, progressive Mexico . . . "

"We did not wish you to think we were failures," came the muttered reply. "You did not warn us of the lawless nature of the country. That is why you are now in honour bound to give us aid . . . "

"I have already told you, Madame, it rests with my ministers." There was an unusual note of acerbity in Louis' voice. "It is up to us now, to get the Emperor out of Mexico as quickly as possible . . . "

"You mean, to abdicate? Never! First you prevail on making him an Emperor . . . and now a yellow, cringing coward!

Never! Never! Never!"

"I will ring for tea," soothed Eugénie.

"Tea? I do not need tea. I need money . . . soldiers . . . "

"Yes, yes. Leave the Emperor's letter with me and I will put it before our ministers," but with every word she uttered, she knew the futility of them all. Mexico's doom was sealed.

It was therefore with great relief that they heard Carlotta was leaving Paris to visit her villa at Miramar. They had other important matters on their mind, for next year would see the realisation of their most ambitious project . . . the Great Universal Exhibition.

★ ★ ★

It was the Prince Imperial's eleventh birthday and Louis had decided the time had come for him to have his own military establishment; three colonels and a naval captain under General Frossard, and an ex-dragoon. Uhlmann, as valet.

The General's first action was to appoint another tutor, for in his eyes, both the behaviour and learning of

France's next Emperor, fell much below standard.

Lou-Lou did not like lessons. His father doted on him and the Court fawned on him; his mother vacillated between criticising one day and spoiling him the next. Only Miss Shaw, now nurse-cum-valet dared to really discipline him.

The new tutor was twenty-five year-old Augustin Filon and though there was spontaneous liking between pupil and tutor, M. Filon was quick to discover he had no easy task.

Having been taught to ride before he could even sit up straight, Lou-Lou was already an expert horseman and nothing pleased him more than to display his prowess before an admiring audience. He was an exhibitionist. He did not know the meaning of fear as M. Filon discovered the afternoon he missed him from the class room. Going to the open window, he saw him making his way along a narrow ledge towards another window. One slip and it would have been instantaneous death on the courtyard below.

Now that the opening of the Paris Exhibition was drawing near, Lou-Lou was busy rehearsing his role, for he was to be the President. As for Eugénie, much of her time was spent in consultation with M. Worth, for lavish entertainment over several months meant more fabulous creations, if she was to maintain her image as the best dressed woman in Europe.

Yet, pervading the air of all the exciting preparations, Eugénie could not get rid of a feeling of guilt.

Carlotta had not stayed long at *Miramar* but had gone to Rome to ask help of the Pope. Of course, he too, had refused, and Carlotta in her anguish had lost her reason and was now back at Miramar, incarcerated in a small summer-house. Were they to blame? Should they have given more help? There was little news from Mexico. First there were rumours Maximilian had decided to abdicate and they had rejoiced. Then came the story he had been persuaded to stay. If only some definite news was forthcoming.

★ ★ ★

As Eugénie, accompanied by the Emperor and the Prince Imperial drove to the opening of the Exhibition, Paris went wild with joy, for Paris was proud to be acting host to the rest of the world. Where else could such a spectacle be seen? The outriders in their green and gold; the postilions in their powdered wigs and tricorn hats and the Cent-Gardes in all their splendour.

The city was bursting at the seams with its influx of visitors; hotels, restaurants, theatres and shops all doing a roaring trade.

At night, the city was full of music, stealing out from grand mansions and restaurants . . . lilting, haunting waltz tunes of Strauss and Offenbach, and the carefree Parisians and their visitors dancing in the boulevards until the early hours of the morning.

Almost every night, either at one of the royal palaces, one of the foreign embassies or the mansion of an important statesman, there was a huge banquet or ball; Eugénie always the centre of admiration ... her painted eyebrows higher than ever ... her hair dusted with powdered gold. Since the opening of the Exhibition, she had taken to having a tall Nubian footman, Scanda, dressed in brilliant silken robes standing behind her chair.

The Prince of Wales and his brother, the Duke of Edinburgh had been early arrivals for Edward had been invited to declare the Exhibition officially open. Unfortunately, Princess Alexandra could not accompany the Prince as she had not fully recovered from the birth of her latest baby.

★ ★ ★

It was going to be a very hot day ... and a very full one. Mentally, Eugénie checked the day's engagements. This morning, a military review for the benefit of the Russians. Then the King of Prussia, accompanied by Bismark was due to arrive in the afternoon and in the evening, a ball at the Russian Embassy.

She pitied the soldiers standing in the heat of the oppressive June day; standing there for hours before the royal party arrived.

She and the ladies remained in their carriages while Louis escorted his guests along the serried ranks of soldiers. She was glad when they left the parade-ground; glad for the sake of the troops. What relief they must feel, as the bands struck up first the Russian national anthem and then *Partant Pour La Syrie* and they could think in terms of comfort of their hard, straw palliasses.

The first carriage, with the perspiring Czar and Louis, flanked by an escort moved away to be followed by Eugénie and the Prince Imperial. Smilingly, she acknowledged the cheers of her people who were obviously cold-shouldering the Czar.

It was then she became aware of some commotion in the escort; a breaking of the ranks, as Captain Raimbaut, leader of the escort, pushed his horse close up to the Imperial carriage. At the same moment, there was a pistol-shot . . . a struggle and a man was dragged away.

Who was the assassin? Whose life did he seek? The procession put on speed, making for the Elysée. By the time Eugénie had dismounted from her carriage, an angry scene was taking place in the hallway of the palace.

"You invite us here to Paris to be your guests, then fail to give us adequate security," the Czar was raving, "Whether it was you or me, he aimed to kill, is immaterial . . . "

Louis was doing his utmost to placate the outraged ruler, but with little success. "We return to Russia this very night." It was then a police officer entered and whispered to Louis. Louis cleared his throat. "The assassin admits to being a Polish exile . . . " he began.

"That is of no account. That he was allowed to get so near the royal carriage . . . "

Eugénie stepped forward. "Sir. I can understand your feelings. Admittedly, we are at fault but I am proud a French officer was instrumental in saving your life at the risk of his own. Please reconsider. Do not return home as yet . . . if only to gratify a sentimental woman."

The Czar was won over. That night at the Russian Embassy Ball, he scarce left her side. Moreover, Louis had given orders that all security measures had to be strengthened for visiting royalty. Pray God, there would be no more attempts of assassination.

★ ★ ★

The summit of the Exhibition had now been reached . . . the awarding of the prizes, for France had given generously to encourage exhibitors.

Eugénie and Louis were to grace the ceremony, M. Worth having created an afternoon gown specially for the occasion. She would be glad when it was over . . . the last official function and they would be free to escape to Biarritz and leave Paris to get on with its entertaining.

She looked up in surprise when Louis entered her dressing-room, his face ashen. In his hand he held a telegram.

"What is it?" she asked hoarsely, at the same time taking it in her own shaking hands. Her senses reeled as she read. It couldn't be. She went back to the beginning to read again. Maximilian had been executed before a firing squad.

212

She looked up at Louis, her face now as white as his.

"What are we going to do?" she asked pitiably.

"Do? There is nothing now that we can do."

"I mean . . . the prize-giving . . . ?"

"Damnation to the prize-giving. No . . . I suppose we must attend."

"I cannot Louis . . . I cannot . . . "

The surprise of seeing Eugénie in a state of weakness increased his own courage.

"We must see this through together, chérie. Then we can take a rest."

"I shall never rest again." Suddenly, she began sobbing uncontrollably. "It was not my fault, Louis, was it? Tell me it was not my fault."

"No, chérie, it was not your fault. There was ample time for Maximilian to have got out of the country . . . as we advised." As though to convince himself, he repeatedly murmured, "No, it was not our fault . . . not our fault . . . "

But in the days that followed, Eugénie knew she would never be able to rid herself of guilt for the part she had played in the tragedy.

She it was who had brought Maximilian and Hidalgo together; she it was who had urged Maximilian and Carlotta to embark on the venture, but France now needed the money and soldiers for her own defence. Prussia was making vast military preparations. France must be ready.

12

HOW had Prince Leopold of Hohenzollern dared to accept the Spanish throne? The French government was loud in its denunciation; Eugénie almost beside herself with fury.

"This is a deliberate insult to France! Germany knew we would never agree to a Prussian on the throne of Spain . . ."

Louis attempted to soothe her. "Have no fear. We shall insist King Wilhelm advises the prince to withdraw."

Leopold needed no advising, becoming aware of the furore he was causing throughout Europe.

Louis was content. "You see, chérie. A little diplomacy . . . a little plain speaking . . ."

Eugénie however would not let the matter drop. "It is not enough. France has been humiliated."

"What more would you ask?"

"The promise that the prince never again seeks to occupy the Spanish throne."

"You cannot dictate to kings and princes . . . "

Nevertheless, King Wilhelm was again approached, but as Louis had anticipated, refused to discuss the matter. It was then Chancellor Bismark acted. For a long time he had sought an opportunity to really provoke France. Accordingly, he altered the King's reply, dissembling the words, so that the reply sounded insolent and arrogant.

The effect on the French ministers and Eugénie was just what Bismark hoped for. This was the final humiliation! France had been insulted before the whole world! France must put Prussia in her place.

"If we do not go to war now," stormed Eugénie, "we are merely postponing it. *Peace bought at the price of disorder would be a great misfortune. This is my war.*"

Louis knew that his hope for a peaceful solution was now fruitless. The government had whipped up the people into clamouring for Prussian blood and on July 19th, 1870, France declared war on Prussia.

* * *

Paris was in a fever of excitement.
Battalions of infantry and troops of
cavalry passing through the city . . . marching
towards the frontier. Crowds of frenzied
onlookers, cheering and waving; hysterical
girls running out into the roadway, to
throw their arms around a soldier . . . any
soldier, to kiss him and to be dragged
along, in her endeavour to keep up
with his quick marching pace, and
above all the loud enthusiastic singing
of the Marseillaise.

It was the same in the café's and
restaurants, orchestras rendering bach's
latest hits, as swaggering officers dined
and wined 'gay ladies', who in return
stuck flowers in their escorts' lapels, and
sprayed them with perfume. The prospect
of war was all so exciting, exhilarating,
intoxicating.

* * *

The Imperial family was in residence at
Fontainbleu, and here too the excitement
was intense, as throughout each day,

217

statesmen and high ranking officers, came to discuss plans for the campaign.

Louis was to be Commander-in-Chief of all the armies, but he showed no enthusiasm whatever, for any of the quick, decisive master-strokes suggested by his generals.

When he was alone with Eugénie, he groaned, "I am too old . . . much too ill and quite unfit to go campaigning."

He saw the look of contempt in her eyes. "You have consistently refused proper medical attention . . . an operation . . . to do so now . . . "

"I know. I know," he interrupted. "Have no fear, I will not give either the army nor the country the opportunity to dub me a coward."

The happiest person at Fontainbleu was the Prince Imperial. Recently on the occasion of his fourteenth birthday, his father had commissioned him as a sous-lieutenant of the Infantry of the line. Now by dint of coaxing, he had persuaded his parents to be allowed to accompany his father to the war zone. Louis, at first had been horrified. "He is but fourteen . . . a child . . . "

"But he does not lack courage. As the future Emperor of France, the experience will be invaluable."

Eugénie's voice was cold. As before, she was to be Regent during Louis' absence. The prospect was exciting; the responsibility greater than ever . . . a challenge, and Mons. Filon, barred from accompanying the Prince was to be her secretary.

★ ★ ★

The farewell assembly was an unforgettable sight; the men in military uniform, their tunics ablaze with decorations and ribbons, while the ladies, gorgeously gowned as usual, chatted together as though they hadn't a care in the world.

At the dining-table Prince Louis was seated between Marquinita and Chiquita, adoration in their eyes as they gazed at their cousin, about to go off to war; now proudly strutting about in his military uniform, the long-waisted tunic unbuttoned to display the red waist-coat and broad blue sash. Every now and again, he would come to a standstill, inserting two fingers of his left hand between the buttons on the waistcoat and adopting the well-known stance of the first Emperor Napoleon, much to the delight and applause of the gathering. Only the Emperor remained silent; too dejected to join in the general hullaballoo.

Throughout the evening, military bands and orchestras had been playing a selection of martial music. Suddenly with a loud roll of drums and a clash of cymbals, the music ended. Then the band-leaders were seen to raise their batons once again . . . hold them . . . then bring them down to the opening bars of the Marseillaise, and there they were, dukes and duchesses, staid statesmen and their ladies, singing the old national anthem, tears streaming down their faces. Then the footmen were joining in, their voices full of fervour and loyalty.

Allons enfants de la patrie,
Le jour de gloire est arrivée.
Contre nous de la tyrannie,
L'étendard sanglant est levé.'

Far into the night, the singing and jubilation continued; the Prince Imperial most energetic of all.

★ ★ ★

The moment of farewell had come. To the Prince's intense disappointment, there had been no ceremonial escort from Fontainbleu. Instead, the royal family had driven to the railway station in pony-traps and carriages.

Eugénie herself had driven the first trap, with the Emperor, wearing the uniform of a marshal seated beside her but the people's cheers died in their throats when they saw him, huddled up in pain, staring straight ahead, ignoring all his well-wishers. Yet apart from giving him an occasional glance of impatience, Her Majesty appeared quite gay.

On the station platform, Louis persisted in ignoring everyone; but the Prince excited as ever, was going around shaking hands; acknowledging salutes and kissing his mother's ladies, not forgetting Chiquita and Marquinita.

It was only when the Prince came to

bid farewell to his mother, that a change came over his face looking as though he was about to burst into tears.

Eugénie, calm and collected, momentarily embraced him, made the sign of the cross on his forehead, and pushed him onto the train.

Now at the window, the train about to start, the Prince had regained his smile. As the engine gave a preliminary snort, and then a slow chugging, Eugénie darted forward calling loudly, "Louis, do your duty." Then she turned away, lest he should see her tears, knowing how near he had been to breaking down. The heir to the French Empire must learn to hide his feelings . . . even though his heart was breaking.

★ ★ ★

As the train rattled on its way to Metz Louis and the generals discussed the opening stage of their campaign. The Metz army would be awaiting them in full strength, for it was now nine days since the declaration of war. They would lose no time, but would march directly into Prussian territory. Within a few days, they would be joined by the Austrian army, and from then on, a joint march to Berlin.

Louis' confidence began to return. It was this damnable pain, that sapped his courage. Now, he told himself, once hostilities were over, and 'Prussia put in her place' as Eugénie phrased it, he would seriously consider having the operation, but until then, he could not spare the time, nor even give his mind to the matter.

They were nearing Metz. The train slowed down. It was running alongside the platform and as Louis gazed through the window, so he was rudely awakened from his day-dream.

There were soldiers everywhere, some asleep on the few benches, others sprawling around on the bare platform, dirty and ill-kempt.

The Imperial party alighting from the train stared first in amazement, which swiftly changed to anger and outraged indignity.

A few of the soldiers recognising the uniforms as high ranking officers, slowly rose to their feet and came to attention, but others deliberately maintained their indolent positions, defiance in their eyes.

An officer stepped forward. "To your feet. Everyone of you. To attention!" The loud, authoritative military command was not to be disobeyed. Now every soldier was standing stiffly to attention, regardless of undone buttons and bare heads.

"The meaning of this? We would have an explanation?"

A non-commissioned officer came to the salute. "Sir. We are in search of our regiments . . . "

"And this is the way you seek them . . . "

"Sir. The men are hungry and tired. Over the last week, they have been moved from one place to another. Then back again, still unable to find their regiments. The barracks are full. There are no spare tents . . . little or no food . . ."

Louis could not restrain his impatience to get down to work, calling a staff meeting the same night. It was a cruel, bitter eye-opener. Far from being 'ready to the last gaiter button', the French army appeared to be in a complete state of chaos.

There were cannon, but no horses to draw them. There was a goodly supply of guns, but a most inadequate amount of ammunition; and all the time, telegrams were pouring in; telegrams from generals requesting destination to assemble their troops; telegrams requesting food, uniforms, medical supplies. The demands were unending.

Day after day Louis attempted some kind of organisation. Then the telegrams from Eugénie began to arrive. 'Why the delay?' 'Why was the army not yet in action?'

The Prince Imperial was also becoming impatient. Daily he would make the same enquiry. "When do we fight, Papa? When is the war going to begin?"

The newspapers too were becoming waspish. Where was that quick decisive victory they had been promised? Something active had to be done.

★ ★ ★

The town of Saarbrücken lay a few miles over the frontier. It was decided that it should be the target of the first French attack.

By now Louis had mobilised an army of over sixty-thousand men, all of whom were to be thrown into battle.

Everyone was now in good spirits. The war would soon be over, and they could return to their homes. As they marched and rode out of Metz led by military bands, the troops frequently burst into the rousing Marseillaise:

> Marchons, marchons
> Qu'un sang impur,
> Abreuvé nos sillons.

Louis and his son accompanied by Uncle Plon-Plon rode in the Imperial carriage, until the actual battle began, then, mounting their horses, rode along with the Voltgeurs.

Prince Louis, was wild with excitement, riding alongside his father, while shells fell around them. Actually, there was little danger, for the Prussians were in full retreat, offering little or no resistance.

That night the French army, settled itself around the town. Tomorrow, they would enter it and push further into enemy territory.

Telegrams and letters were immediately sent to Eugénie and the Parisian newspapers. Now they had something they could print. Louis wrote Eugénie:

'Louis has received his baptism of fire. His coolness was admirable. He showed no emotion, and might have been strolling in the Bois de Boulogne. There were men who shed tears at seeing him so calm.'

It was unbelievable. Overnight, orders had been given that the army was to withdraw back to Metz. Rumour after rumour spread among the men, the chief being that the Emperor, did not yet consider his army powerful enough to march to Berlin.

Then the Prussians struck . . . not at one point, but all along the frontier. It was only two days after Saarbrücken, that news of a major defeat had taken place at Wissenbourg. Then within forty-eight hours, came the defeats at Froeschwiller and Forbach, the armies of Alsace and Lorraine being in full retreat.

Louis was horror-stricken . . . staggered . . . dazed. While aware of the French army's weakness, he had been hoping for a miracle . . . never expecting such immediate disaster. What could he do? His brain was revolving round and round the bitter dread of informing the Empress. At last be dictated a telegram.

'*Our troops are in full retreat. Nothing remains but the defence of the capital.*'

As she read the telegram, Eugénie could scarce control her fury. She might have known, that her gutless, spineless husband would make a complete débâcle of the war. She had suspected it from the beginning when he had written:

'*Nothing is ready. We have not troops enough. I believe we have lost our chance of invading.*'

She had written back, a scathing, sarcastic letter. Was he not the Emperor?

. . . the nephew of the great Emperor Napoleon? He must lose no time, in uniting the armies and stinking!

She could see now, that Saarbrücken had been but a sop to silence her and the French press until . . . until defeat?

She lost no time in calling the Council, and did not hesitate to vent her spleen on the Emperor, much to the embarrassment of her ministers, save a few antagonistic ones, who were quick to agree with her.

"*Let the army be concentrated in the hand of one man . . . but not the Emperor,*" blustered one of them.

"But if he leaves the army, he is dishonoured for ever."

"I agree." It was Eugénie. "He must stay with the army . . . but with someone else in command." Her voice was full of contempt.

"But . . . who do you suggest . . . ?"

"That we will now decide."

At the end of the meeting Eugénie handed a note to Mons. Filon. "Put it in code and despatch to the Emperor immediately."

As Filon set about his task, he felt his blood run cold. How could Her

Majesty send such a cruel letter? With unpremeditated audacity he sought her out in her study.

"Yes? Is there something you don't understand?"

"This letter, Your Majesty. It is horrible . . ."

"It is meant to be. War is horrible. Send the message." But as Filon set it out in code, he sought more gentle, more considerate phrases.

★ ★ ★

Louis stared at the decoded message that had just been handed to him. How could Eugénie do this to him — to humiliate him before his staff, before all France? He closed his eyes to stem the threatened tears, knowing he was going to need all his courage to make the shameful announcement.

Then without looking up, pretending to read, he spoke:

"Her Majesty, the Regent, has deemed it necessary, to make a change. From today, she has appointed Marshal Bazaine to be Commander-in-Chief . . . " He could not go on. No-one round the table, spoke a word, until Louis rose, and with utmost courtesy, continued . . . "and so gentlemen, I leave you in the capable hands of Marshal Bazaine."

It was Bazaine who spoke first. "Sir. I am overwhelmed. I had no idea . . . "

His protest was lost in a sea of commiseration.

"What are your plans, sir?" "Will you be returning to Paris?"

Louis shook his head. "No . . . No. I am a soldier of France. I shall stay . . . "

He couldn't tell them the Empress had forbidden him to return to Paris . . . that he must win a decisive victory or die on the battlefield. Nor would she hear of the Prince Imperial returning home.

★ ★ ★

Bazaine's first action was to move all troops from Metz to Chalôns but halfway there, changed his mind and returned to Metz. Louis however, insisted that he and the Prince Imperial were continuing to Chalôns where the army was under the command of Marshall MacMahon.

There, he found that MacMahon had a suggestion. As the Emperor was no longer in command of the armies, should he not be in command of the Government? Why not send General Trochu to Paris, as the newly appointed Governor, with the message, that the Emperor was following to defend the capital?

Louis was only too willing to listen to any suggestion and eagerly awaited Eugénie's reply.

It came, cold and relentless. If he was to return to Paris, he would be pelted in the streets . . . not with stones but with ordure. The army of Chalôns was to join up with Bazaine at Metz, and he and the Prince Imperial were to proceed with them.

There was nothing Louis could do. He had to obey the Regent's orders, but he knew he was an embarrassment to the army, as MacMahon showed only too clearly, making no arrangements for the Emperor's position in the cavalcade. Thus it was, the Imperial carriage bearing Louis and the Prince found itself, wedged between baggage wagons, and later that evening when they drove into Tourteron, townsfolk and soldiers alike, were amazed to see the Emperor appear from among the baggage wagons. Immediately a cry went up from some uncouth wit "Voila l'Empereur Bagage! Voila l'Empereur Bagage et le petit prince de Bagages!"

There was loud laughter, and the cry was taken up, till the air rang with insult, 'Bagage! Bagage! Bagage!'

Louis had come to a decision, and this time he was not going to consult Eugénie. The Prince Imperial must be taken to safety. For himself he cared nothing; indeed he would welcome death. Louis listened in silence as his father discussed details with Captain Duperré.

"So, my son, you leave tomorrow, for England . . . "

"Yes, papa, yes . . . " Louis' voice was low and submissive.

The Emperor regarded him in surprise. He had expected an outburst of disappointment, but the boy actually seemed relieved! Poor little boy, he thought, he must now be thoroughly disillusioned.

233

★ ★ ★

Louis' physical agony was now so distressing, that his doctors were constantly giving him drugs and sedatives, reducing him to a state of almost constant langour, scarcely aware of what was going on around him, trundling in the wake of Marshal MacMahon, endeavouring to reach Metz.

It was on the morning of September 1st, that MacMahon found himself trapped at Sedan, facing the full power of the Prussian army, with Bazaine nowhere near to give aid. For more than twelve hours the battle raged, the French army hopelessly outnumbered, and out-manoeuvred. Hour after hour, Louis rode about the battlefield, praying for a bullet to hit him, until in the late afternoon, the German artillery having almost wiped out the army from Chalôns, and MacMahon, having been wounded, Louis took command and issued the orders to cease fire.

The white flag was hoisted above the walls of Sedan and Louis sent word of his surrender to the King of Prussia.

'Sire, my brother,

Having been unable to die among my troops, there remains nothing for me to do, but surrender my sword to Your Majesty. I am Your Majesty's good brother,

                              Napoleon.

13

MONS. FILON paced about the Emperor's study in a state of stunned apprehension. On his way to the Tuileries, he had heard the calamitous news. How had the Empress taken it? There was bound to be a scene with her. The sooner it was over, the sooner they could make plans.

He became aware that she was standing at the top of the spiral staircase connecting her study with the Emperor's. He looked up, breathing deeply, waiting.

For a moment she regarded him, wild-eyed, and then her control snapped. "Do you know what they are saying?" she screamed. "They say that he has surrendered . . . capitulated . . . ! You do not believe that, do you?"

With no reply coming from the quaking secretary, she screamed still louder. "You do not believe it do you? Say it . . . say that you do not believe it . . . "

"Your Majesty . . . " came the

stammering voice. "There are times
. . . circumstances . . . when even the
most courageous . . ."

"So you have heard! The craven
poltroon! The dastardly, white-livered
rat! The spiritless dunghill-cock . . ."

Mons. Filon stared . . . transfixed,
mesmerised, as Eugénie went on and
on, progressing from vulgar epithets to
filthy, profane expressions, he had never
before heard from a woman's lips. On
and on went the tirade, her voice hoarse
with agony, wild with fury, Filon, so
shocked, that the vile words made no
lasting imprint on his mind . . . only the
general horror.

She suddenly stopped, holding on to
the iron balustrade with both hands,
just uttering scream after scream, like
a wounded, dying animal, then with a
final 'Cowardly skunk', she turned and
went back to her room.

★ ★ ★

The Tuileries seemed to be almost
deserted. Obviously, the majority of the
Court had already left, but realising the

Empress' overwrought condition, Filon decided to stay the night.

Surprisingly, when he met her the next morning, she was quite calm. She had already held a Council meeting, at which she had been advised to abdicate; a suggestion she had scornfully rejected. She was the Regent, and as such she remained.

The meeting had scarcely broken up, when M. Chevreau, Prefect of Lyons, dashed back into the room, unannounced.

"Your Majesty . . . Your Majesty . . . all is lost. The mob has reached the Palais Bourbon. They're heading for the Tuileries . . ."

"But General Trochu is in charge."

"The General has gone over to the people. They're shouting for the Republic . . . for your abdication . . ."

They were joined by General Mellinet, the general in charge of the Guard. "They're already in the gardens of the Tuileries. Shall I open fire on them, Your Majesty?"

"No. No. I will not be responsible for bloodshed here in the city."

"Then you must escape now . . . before the mob invades the Palace."

"Never. I am the Regent of France, and here I stay."

"But madame, most of the Corps Legislatif have already gone . . . "

"Let them go . . . and all others who wish. I make no demands on their service or loyalty."

They needed no second bidding and within an hour Eugénie found herself alone with M. Filon, Pauline Metternich and her husband; Mme. Lebreton, one of her ladies and Count Nigra, the Italian Ambassador.

Through the open window, they could hear the savage, screaming and shouting.

"Death to the Spanish woman! A bas! Vive la Republique! A mort! A mort!"

She turned to Filon. "Go fetch me a loaded revolver!"

For a moment M. Filon hesitated. What was in Her Majesty's mind? Suicide or self-preservation?

Count Nigra spoke urgently. "If you were to leave now, Your Majesty, you go as Regent . . . "

" . . . and if you remain," added

Prince Metternich, "not only is your life in danger, but that of all who are found here with you."

"It is not death, I'm afraid of," muttered Pauline Metternich, "but the possibility of being raped by one of that scum. Remember it happened to Marie Antoinette's ladies."

"Rape?" For the first time, fear showed in Eugénie's eyes. "Oh, no. Not that. Fetch me a cloak and bonnet." She turned to Prince Metternich. "My jewels which I entrusted to you . . . ?"

"They are safe at the Austrian Embassy . . . "

"Thank God for that." She glanced frantically out of the window, where the mob had increased in size; their shouts and threats louder and more violent, "How can we get out . . . it's impossible . . . and how . . . how can I go alone? And where?"

"I shall be honoured, Your Majesty, if you allow me to accompany you." It was Mme. Le Breton.

Eugénie gave her a fleeting, wan smile of gratitude, as Richard Metternich interposed. "We'll find a way out . . . through the back. There's not a moment to lose."

Through a series of long, tortuous corridors, the existence of which, none had ever previously known, they eventually came out in the Place Saint-Germain. There, the crowds were milling about on the footpaths and no notice was taken of the small group.

Prince Metternich acted quickly, hailing a passing cab, and with complete lack of ceremony, pushed the Empress and her lady within. Eugénie embraced Pauline, tears in her eyes, as Richard spoke guardedly. "Drive straight to one of your friends, and get away to England as quickly as you can . . . and God go with you."

Eugénie looked hopelessly at her lady. "To whom shall we go? Almost all my ladies have deserted me."

They tried several of the magnificent mansions, but all appeared to be locked up and their owners fled. Eugénie was fast becoming hysterical until Mme. Le Breton suggested. "Why not try M. Evans, the American dentist? He is a lifelong friend of the Emperor?"

Dr. Evans was at home, but when he

recognised the two ladies who had refused to give their names to the footman, he too appeared alarmed and perturbed.

Looking around to ensure they were not being observed, he quickly ushered them into a small room. "I am entertaining a party of men to dinner . . . all ardent Republicans. It would never do for them to find you here."

Eugénie could not restrain her tears. "You will be perfectly safe in here," soothed the doctor, "I will lock the door, to prevent anyone wandering in."

It was several hours before he could rejoin them, and then it was to find the Empress in a state of frenzy.

"What is to become of me? Even here, I can hear them screaming for my blood."

"I will get you away, Your Majesty. Only trust me."

"But my son? Where is my son? Is he alive?"

"By now, Your Majesty, I expect he is safe in England. The Emperor was most wise in sending him to safety, before . . ."

"The only wise thing he ever did. And

where is he now? Resting safe and sound in prison . . . while I am fleeing for my life. Why couldn't he have taken the honourable way out, and put a bullet through his brain. Oh, I am so hungry . . . so very hungry . . ."

"Yes, Your Majesty, yes, but I dare not let any of my servants know that you are here. I will fetch food now. Then you must try to sleep, for I intend to get you out of Paris before the city is awake . . ."

★ ★ ★

The brougham dashing along the highway to Deauville, suddenly slowed down, as several soldiers stepped into the road. Passing through villages and hamlets, they had become accustomed to the cries of 'Vive la Republique' but this was the first time they had been halted.

The coachman bent down, and in a conspiratorial voice mouthed, "Taking a patient into the country," at the same time tapping his forehead, "Bad mental case."

"Your papers?" came the laconic demand.

Dr. Evans produced the necessary documents, for himself and his valet Spode, up on the box with him, and for the sick woman and her companion. Having scrutinised the papers, the man put his head through the carriage window. "Sacre-bleu! She looks a right wild-eyed loon. I wish you joy with her," and stepped aside making ribald jests with his companions.

With a sigh of relief Dr. Evans drove on to Deauville. Pray God, he would be successful in finding a ship to take them across the Channel.

★ ★ ★

Not for many years could even hardened sailors remember such a storm as swent the channel that night, but Sir Jolin Burgoyne, owner of the yacht *Gazelle* had gallantly given his promise to Eugénie not to put back to Deauville.

When the storm-tossed vessel eventually landed at Ryde, the Empress, bruised and dazed as she was, insisted on landing

244

immediately in the hope of having news of the Prince Imperial.

Accommodation was secured at the George Hotel, and while the ladies settled themselves to rest, the doctor went out in search of information.

To his delight, this was immediately forthcoming, for buying a newspaper, big headlines met his eyes. The Prince Imperial had landed at Hastings and was staying at the Marine Hotel together with his aide-de-camp and valet.

Racing back Dr. Evans dashed up to Eugénie's room, banging on the door, "Your Majesty! Your Majesty, the Prince is in England . . . at Hastings."

The door was opened with such violence that the doctor almost fell into the room. "Is it true? Really true? How long will it take us to get to Hastings?" Eugénie's fists beat upon Dr. Evans' chest, tears streaming down her cheeks.

He led her back into the room. "I think it would be wiser, Madame, if you were to rest for a few hours . . ."

"No . . . No . . . We must go now . . . immediately."

245

Realising the futility of reasoning with her, they crossed over to the mainland with as little delay as possible and then on to Hastings.

* * *

The Marine Hotel made no claims to pretentiousness, but with a Royal guest under its roof, the manager felt he could afford to be patronising towards the four travel-stained foreigners seeking accommodation.

"No, sir we have no vacant rooms . . ."

"Then would you please take us up to the Prince Imperial . . . "

"Indeed, sir, No. The Prince does not wish to see anyone . . . "

It was too much for Eugénie. "Out of my way. I insist we go up," and calling up her last reserve of strength, pushed by the astounded manager.

It was then, that a door, on the first floor opened and the Prince stepped out, "Maman! Maman! I heard your voice. Oh Maman! Maman!"

They were in each others arms, their tears intermingling; Mme. Le Breton, weeping on Dr. Evans' shoulder, while Spode, found himself being handed keys of rooms, which the manager had suddenly found were vacant after all.

★ ★ ★

The news of their safe arrival had reached France, resulting in the Duke of Alba, accompanied by Marquinita and Chiquita, joining them.

Then came Mons. Filon, Dr. Conneau and his son, together with a number of other loyal Imperialists, but it was the arrival of Pauline Metternich, that brought home to Eugénie, the enormity of her great loss; and it was she who approached the Empress' position in a practical manner.

After the first greetings and tears were over, Pauline asked, "Have you any money, Your Majesty?"

Eugénie shook her head. "None whatever. I never thought of it. There are my jewels. They must be sold."

"And until then, you must accept a loan from me."

"How good you are . . . "

247

"And this hotel is no place for you and the Prince . . ."

"Where else can we go?"

"Filon must look around. Visit estate agencies . . . nearer to London. There are many suitable mansions on the outskirts."

★ ★ ★

It was odd, but since the nightmare dash from the Tuileries, and the dreadful Channel crossing, ending with the joyous reunion with her son, a change had come over Eugénie.

Had she been too hard on Louis? She had since heard of his courage at Sedan, and now that he was a prisoner at Wilhelshöhe, she had written to him, letters full of compassion for his present position and hope for the future.

It was the middle of September before she received a reply . . . a letter of equal tenderness.

'The affectionate expressions in your letters have done me a world of good, for I was much grieved by your *silence . . . Your letters are a wonderful consolation, and I thank you for them. To what can I attach myself if it is not your affection and that of our son.'*

In her next letter she asked where should they live when he was liberated? She suggested Trieste, where they had a villa, but Louis wrote back.

' . . . we can be happy only in free countries like England and Switzerland. When I am free, I want to come and live with you and Louis in a little cottage with bow windows and creepers . . . '

By the end of September, Eugénie had found a house, Camden Place, in Chislehurst, where she quickly gathered a court around her, gradually assuming, on a small scale, the atmosphere of St. Cloud . . . even the old-time faithful servants; Pepa, her personal maid; Ferrand, the head chef; Girard, the butler; Schmidt, a palace footman and De'lafosse, the maître d'hôtel from the Tuileries.

The Duc de Bassano, too had arrived

to take his place as Chamberlain to the household.

Then began the arrival of Imperialistic families, renting or buying houses in the vicinity, convinced that it was merely a matter of a short time before the Republic would be overthrown. In the meantime, they wished to retain their positions near the Emperor and Empress, for there were indications that in the very near future, the peace treaty would be signed and the Emperor given his liberty.

★ ★ ★

Outside Camden House, the thick November fog swirled across the lawns, obliterating all hope of seeing the carriages when they turned into the drive, yet Eugénie's spirits were soaring high. Today, Her Majesty, Queen Victoria was coming to visit her. Since her arrival in England, the Prince and Princess of Wales had called on several occasions. So had other royalties, but the Queen had kept distinctly aloof. When the sound of wheels on the frost-hardened gravel announced her arrival, Eugénie was at the door, with her ladies and gentlemen behind her and the Prince Imperial at her side.

The Queen was accompanied by Princess Beatrice, now thirteen years old, a true Hanoverian with fair complexion and long plaits hanging down her back. Having been presented to the Empress, she smilingly handed her a nosegay, Victoria in the meantime busy appraising Louis from toe to head. "So you are Louis! The perfect little Frenchman, I see."

Conversation was difficult with the two children in the room; Louis standing stiffly by the Queen's chair, and Beatrice sitting beside Eugénie. While their elders talked guardedly of the war, each remembering Victoria's two daughters married to Prussians, Beatrice and Louis frequently found themselves staring at each other, and then shyly looking away.

The Queen took her leave after only half an hour's visit, but inviting Eugénie and Louis to visit her at Windsor the following week.

As the carriage rolled away, Eugénie

was lost in deep thought. She had seen those glances exchanged between Louis and Beatrice. Supposing . . . just supposing . . . It would be an excellent match . . . some difficulty about religion . . . but an excellent match.

★ ★ ★

Eugénie, with Louis by her side in the long string of carriages approaching Dover harbour, gasped in amazement. She had never anticipated there would be a crowd to watch the arrival of an exiled emperor. Had they come to mock and deride?

She was glad of the protection of the policemen, who encircled her and the Imperial party as they made their way to the quayside. Ever since she had heard of the Emperor's impending release, a strange feeling had been growing within her . . . she was longing for his return . . . longing to care for him . . . to cherish him.

The Prince too was beaming with joy. Papa was coming home. Papa who he had left on the battlefield; almost dead with pain and exhaustion.

The steamer was now alongside; the gangway down, and as Eugénie strained to catch the first glimpse of her husband, her heart almost stood still. Dear God, was that little old man, with the sparse, tufty white hair, Louis Napoleon? She watched him treading carefully, almost fearfully, his face pale; his eyes more puffy than ever. Then it happened. From the crowd behind her, rose a volume of loud cheers. Louder and louder it grew. Now flowers were being thrown. Louis stopped . . . bewildered. Why this welcome for him? Then he saw Eugénie, and quickened his step.

She was in his arms, mingling her tears with his; returning kiss for kiss. He had always loved her, but never more than in this moment. Never in all his married life had she kissed him with such unrestrained joy.

The crowd was howling with delight. To see royalty caught up in such tense emotion, was an experience of a lifetime. Then Louis became aware of a tugging; a pushing; and a mock plaintive voice, "I am here, too, Papa."

Louis caught his son up to him, holding both him and Eugénie in a tight embrace, as police endeavoured to push a way back to the waiting carriages. As they progressed, handkerchiefs fluttered on both sides, and hats and walking sticks were thrown up in the air. A truly royal welcome.

It was the same when they arrived back at Chislehurst; the villagers coming out from their cottages to wave and cheer and throw spring flowers into the carriage.

It was late into the night, before Louis and Eugénie found themselves alone.

"Now that you are free, we can go ahead with our plans." There was the old urgency in Eugénie's voice.

"Plans?" he queried dully.

"For your return to France. To oust the Republicans . . . "

As if he had not heard her, almost as if talking to himself, he muttered, "The Tuileries . . . St. Cloud . . . the hotel de Ville . . . all burned to the ground . . . "

"Yes . . . Yes . . . but we can rebuild . . . "

He shook his head. "No. We have lost

254

the throne of France. Robbed our son of his birthright."

"Never, Louis. Never. There is a meeting here tomorrow of our Imperialistic friends. You have only to listen and you will marvel at their passionate zeal. Being imprisoned may have dulled your ambition but you must look ahead for the sake of Louis, our son, the next Emperor of France, Napoleon IV."

"Still my hopeful, aspiring Eugénie, yet all I ask is to be with you and Louis here at Camden House." She suddenly noticed a broad smile on his face.

"What is it you find so amusing?"

"I was thinking of when I last visited this house . . . "

"You have been in this house before . . . when?"

"During my last exile." The smile broadened still more. "I wooed the daughter of the house, Miss Emily Rowles . . . "

"I should have known there was a woman in the story . . . " she said banteringly.

"It was all very proper and correct. Although Papa and Mama were in full approval, the young lady and I were never allowed to be alone together . . ."

"The young lady had wise parents. But what was the outcome?"

He hesitated. "Well . . . the choice lay between marrying the lady and her Papa's money and living in England for the rest of my life . . . or remaining an impoverished exile with the hope that someday . . . "

"You would become the Emperor of France? And you did, Louis, you did! And you will do it again, *mon amour* and then, ah then, Louis, we will rebuild Paris, more beautiful than ever."

14

EIGHTEEN months had elapsed since Louis had joined Eugénie in exile .. months of apparently standing still ... regaining confidence and composure, gaining for the first time a new, tender relationship. The friendship of the Queen and her family was of tremendous help to them both; indeed Victoria was once again full of ardent admiration for Louis *'so brave and dignified in his terrible misfortunes.'*

But beneath the pleasant façade of family life, and the miniature French Court at Camden House, there was an air of suppressed activity about the place ... unsuspected by the outside world. As at the Tuileries, Eugénie held a salon each Sunday, when she and her ladies and guests floated around in their gorgeous dresses ... for M. Worth visited Camden House frequently; listening to the singers and pianists engaged for their entertainment. There were however, other visitors, ardent Imperialists, and they came to discuss plans and schemes. At first Louis had been indifferent, but he had soon been caught up in their enthusiasm and optimism, and was now chafing to put their plans into operation.

Today, on the Queen's invitation they were attending a military review at Bushey Park, Louis and Eugénie watching from their carriage, with the Prince riding alongside. Eugénie's eyes lit up with pleasure, when a messenger brought the request, Prince Louis should join the Queen. She watched them chatting; Louis with perfect ease; Victoria all smiles; Beatrice listening, eyes downcast until he rode round to her side of the carriage, then her face radiating girlish excitement.

"It would be such a good match, would it not Louis?" sighed Eugénie.

"*Ma chérie*. You are as keen a matchmaker as your mother. I cannot see the Queen giving her daughter to an exiled Prince."

"But not an exile for much longer. Ah, Louis I can scarcely wait for Spring."

He shook his head. "You are too impatient, and when the time does come, who can foretell the result?"

"We shall defeat the Republicans. Nothing is more certain. We must for Louis' sake . . . we must."

It was after dinner that night, that Louis summoned the Prince into his study.

"I am not very happy about your progress with M. Filon."

"I am sorry Papa. I know . . . I do not like lessons. It is not the fault of M. Filon," he added hurriedly.

Louis regarded his son with a twinkle in his eye. "I am glad you are aware of your shortcomings. However, I have now made other arrangements for you."

The Prince looked alarmed. "You are not sending me to a school, sir?"

"Yes. That is just what I am doing." For a moment he watched the boy's rising consternation and then added " . . . To the Royal Military Academy at Woolwich."

"Papa! Really! Oh thank you, Papa. Ever since I visited the Academy a month ago, I have envied the fellows there. When do I go?"

"As soon as we collect your uniforms and equipment. Louis Conneau is to accompany you."

"You think of everything Papa. I should hate to be parted from him."

"A house has been taken for you, with M. Filon in charge. Uhlmann, will of course go as your valet and there will be a couple of maids and a footman. Your first establishment!"

The boy's face beamed with pleasure. "I am longing to wear uniform again. What rank do I have, sir?"

"That of a gentleman cadet. Twelve hours of study and drill each day and no privileges."

★ ★ ★

Not much longer now, and they would be riding into Paris. Plon-Plon had taken a house in London, and visited the Emperor almost every day, determined not to be left out. By now, Louis was totally convinced that the attempt could not fail.

By way of Switzerland, accompanied

by the Prince Imperial and Plon-Plon, he was to make a secret entry into Lyons, where the Commander-in-Chief of the Southern armies was a Bonaparte sympathiser. There the army would proclaim him Emperor of France, and then would begin the victorious march on Paris. Having established himself at the Louvre, Eugénie and her ladies would lose no time in joining him and the Prince.

A date in March had been fixed for the great venture. The Prince had not been told, lest in his youthful impetuosity, he should betray the plan, but Eugénie's joy at the prospect of returning to Paris was obvious to all her entourage.

Only one matter was giving Louis any real concern. How would he fare on the long ride from Lyons to Paris? Memories of the agony he suffered during those weeks of war were constantly with him.

He had come to a decision. He would have the operation, his doctors had so long been advocating. Then there would be plenty of time before March for convalescence.

Surprisingly, the doctors suggested they

should try treatment in preference to surgery, and at first, their efforts met with success.

Prince Louis had several days leave at Christmas, preening himself before his parents and their guests in his English military uniform, much to the delight of the ladies who insisted trying on those very *chic chapeaux*, first the blue and gold pill-box, and then the busby with its stiff white plume. The atmosphere was electric in its gaiety; a foretaste of what life would be at the Louvre.

It was early in the New Year that the severe pain returned and Louis demanded the London surgeon, Sir Henry Thomson be called in to perform the operation.

On January 2nd Sir Henry operated, removing a large stone from the bladder, but unfortunately there were other fragments to be removed at a later date when the Emperor regained his strength.

Daily, messages and enquiries were pouring in from the Queen and other members of the Royal Family. The surgeon was hopeful, and on January 6th performed a second operation again successfully, so that he prepared for still another, on the 9th.

The operation was to take place at noon. To ensure a good night's sleep, Louis had been heavily sedated, and was still dazed the following morning, but able to talk to Dr. Conneau who was sitting by his bedside.

His voice was feeble. "*Where is Louis?*"

"*At Woolwich, sir. Shall I send for him?*"

"*No. He's at work. He must not be disturbed.*" His voice had become almost a whisper. "*Conneau, dear friend, we were not cowards at Sedan, were we?*"

"Indeed, no, sir . . . you especially, fought most courageously."

Sir Henry entered the room, and glancing at his patient was startled at the change that had come over him.

"Give him some brandy and water, while I fetch the Empress," he gasped.

He overtook Eugénie as she was about to leave the house.

"Madame . . . there is a minor crisis. I would advise you not to leave the

263

house, Colonel Clary has gone to fetch the Prince."

She stared at him dully as though she did not understand, and then without speaking followed him back upstairs.

As they approached the Emperor's bedroom, the door opened and one of the doctors rushed out, calling for a priest.

Eugénie was on her knees by the bedside, her hands taking those of the Emperor. "It is Eugénie . . . Louis . . . your Empress. Louis is coming."

A smile hovered about his lips, but as the priest came forward to administer the last sacrament, Eugénie sobbed. "*C'est impossible . . . C'est impossible,*" praying incoherently.

It was Dr. Conneau who gently told her the Emperor had passed away. Letting out a wild scream, she stumbled to her feet, gazing down on the now relaxed face of Louis. Then drawing in a deep, steadying breath, she kissed him first on the forehead and then on both cheeks.

Sadly the doctor went down to the front of the house, to await the arrival of The Prince Imperial, now Louis Napoleon IV.

The boy did not need to be told, rushing upstairs with such haste, he stumbled several times. As he entered his father's room, Eugénie turned, clutching him to her, whimpering, "*I have nothing left now Louis, only you*," but releasing himself, he fell on his knees by the bedside, gasping out the Lord's Prayer, until his sobbing choked the words, and he was able to assuage his grief in a torrent of weeping.

★ ★ ★

Louis Napoleon III had been laid to rest at the little nearby church of St. Mary's. No pompous military funeral, but nevertheless, an immense following of mourners lead by the Prince Imperial, the Prince of Wales and the Duke of Edinburgh. Then came thousands of loyal Imperialists, of both high and low degree, and hundreds of humble-folk from the surrounding countryside who had come to love the gentle, courteous 'old gentleman' as they had dubbed him.

Eugénie remained in her darkened room, not emerging until the next day, when the will was read. Then the storm broke. Everything had been left to her. Plon-Plon raved like a mad-man, insisting a search should be made for a later-dated will, but all to no avail.

"Louis himself told me he was naming me as the next leader of the Bonapartes . . . " he stormed.

Ridiculous! How could he, with young Louis . . . Eugénie had now cast aside all her grief, forced into action to fight for her son's rights.

"He is not yet of age . . . "

"No, but remember, I left France as the Regent. I can go back as Regent . . . "

"Do you think you are a fit person to school him to sit on the throne of France?"

"Your impertinence, sir, at such a time, belittles you still more in my eyes."

"Someone has destroyed that will!" Now Plon-Plon was becoming menacing. "I demand, that according to the Emperor's last wishes, I take the Prince back to France; to have sole responsibility for his upbringing."

"How dare you! The Emperor would

never make such a condition."

Ignoring her outburst he went on, " . . . and that I shall have sole control of the Imperialistic party . . . "

"I should be glad if you would leave my house, sir." For once, she was able to control her fiery temper. The very thought of Louis being taken from her having numbed her brain ice-cold.

Long after he had gone, she still sat there. How would the Bonaparte faction now fare? Would her son ever sit on the throne of France? Departing Imperialists, had that morning, re-assured that they would never rest, until once again there was a French Empire. Tears ran down her cheeks. She doubted it, but she must be ready. Louis must be ready. The thought of never again living in Paris was too horrible to contemplate.

In the meantime, he must continue at Woolwich. There, she told herself, he would have the finest opportunity of aquiring leadership. Then when the call came, he would be ready.

15

THROUGH the recommendation of the Queen, Louis had been allowed to join a Battery at Aldershot. Now he was a professional soldier . . . but how, when and where would he ever be able to show his prowess?

While on holiday in Switzerland, staying at their villa Arenenberg, he had thought it a good opportunity to write offering his services to Emperor Franz Joseph of Austria, and here was a letter from His Imperial Majesty declining the offer.

"But Louis," Eugénie spoke consolingly, "cannot you understand? You are a Frenchman. Your taking up arms against any other European country, could cause a serious breach."

When he refused to listen to her reasoning, she tried a different approach. "We go back to England, next week," she began.

"To what? The same old round of house-parties. The same bored wives chasing me, calling me 'their little boy'. The same mamas gushing over me while their lady-like daughters hang their heads and dare not speak."

Eugénie laughed. "You are in a bad mood, Louis. I thought you enjoyed the house-parties . . . that you were the life and soul . . . "

"Everything becomes boring when you have a surfeit . . . "

She looked at him shrewdly. "The cure for your boredom would be marriage . . . "

"Oh, Maman, please, please do not bring up that subject again. I have repeatedly told you, I do not as yet wish to have my wings clipped."

"You are nearly twenty-three. The Prince of Wales was married at a much earlier age."

"Is he a good advertisement for marriage?"

"He is one of your dearest friends. You are constantly in his company."

"That is not to say I approve of his behaviour."

"But seriously, Louis, if you delay

much longer, in asking the Queen for the hand of Beatrice . . . you may lose her."

"Really Mama, you are the most persistent of matchmakers. What do I really know of Princess Beatrice? She is charming, pretty, and when I speak with her, I find her intelligent, but remember, Maman, there is always a lady in attendance, to hear all we say. We can never talk alone . . . never really know each other."

"That would come after marriage."

"Never. I *refuse to stoop to the part a princely commercial traveller . . . to view the princesses and boast my expectations . . .*"

She tried another line of approach, "But all men need a woman in their lives," she coaxed.

" . . . or women," he laughed, noting her quick dismay.

"Are there other women?" she probed.

"Wouldn't you like to know, Maman? I run a positive harem. All those ladies I meet up and down the country at the house-parties; at the London assemblies. I am the world's worst philanderer."

"I do not believe you. If it were true, the Queen would not encourage your friendship with her daughter. When we get back to Camden House, I shall ask Arthur Bigge. He will tell me the truth."

"Will he? He is my closest friend. He would never betray me."

She approved of his friendship with Arthur Bigge. They had met when he had gone to Aldershot, and along with two other young officers, Lieutenants Slade and Wodehouse, they made up an inseparable quartet, visiting Camden House most weekends, much to her enjoyment. When Marquinita and Chiquita married Spanish dukes, their visits to England had ceased, leaving her and Louis desolate, a desolation that was heightened the following year, when dear little Chiquita had died in childbirth.

Were there any women in Louis' life. She knew he had rooms in London, and often stayed overnight. Had he a mistress? The possibility haunted her. Would he eventually become as his father; as the Prince of Wales? Then again she had caught fragments of talk between the young men, about the 'gay ladies of Leicester Square'; talk that always ended abruptly when they became aware of her presence.

Louis had inherited her fiery Spanish nature; her impulsiveness, with the result that his behaviour was often rash, excitable, even wilful, as hers had been in younger days.

From his father had come his charm; charm that the ladies could not resist, from Her Majesty the Queen down to the Camden House maidservants.

She was proud of him; proud that the Prince and Princess of Wales, included him in their 'set'; proud that all the important families clamoured for his company, but most of all she was proud of his courage. He did not know the meaning of fear, and at times, although he was something of an exhibitionist, his actions invariably proved that he was no braggart.

Please God, the day might not be too far away, when he would sit on the throne of France.

★ ★ ★

Throughout the Autumn and Winter, Eugénie was considerably surprised at Louis' behaviour, refusing all invitations to house-parties and balls.

As the weeks went by, her curiosity could not be contained. "Why Louis? Why? Your refusals will be giving offence."

He had shrugged his shoulders. "They bore me."

"But you were the originator of the wildest practical jokes . . ."

"Maman! I am past the stage of practical jokes. I want more out of life . . ."

Of course it meant that she saw more of him and his three friends. Sometimes she joined in their conversations; serious conversations . . . chiefly dealing with the political affairs of Europe and she was amazed at the depth of their arguments and knowledge.

Over Christmas, their main topic was the war in South Africa against the Zulus.

"Nothing but a horde of savages," scoffed Lieutenant Slade.

"But well trained savages," put in Arthur Bigge.

Louis eyes were dreamy. "It would be an ideal war for me. I must not participate in any European conflict, say my party, but in Africa against savages, they could not object."

"Ideal war? Horrible war." It was Arthur Bigge again. "They are a cruel race. They take no prisoners."

"Is it true, that having killed, they disembowel their victims?" Lieutenant Wodehouse's voice was a mixture of curiosity and awe.

"Only too true."

It was towards the end of January that they learned just how true. The Zulus had made a surprise attack on the British, almost wiping out a complete regiment, leaving over a thousand soldiers disembowelled on the field.

The English government was furious. Large reinforcements must be sent out immediately. Louis' friends were among the first to go, leaving the Prince miserable and envious. "Why couldn't I go?" he stormed.

"Because the English government would never allow it," Eugénie attempted to placate him, but his moods and behaviour were making Camden House a very uncomfortable place.

There came the evening when Eugénie had to protest. "Louis, for goodness sake, please try to sit still. You are most distracting, first jumping out of your chair, walking about, strumming a few notes on the piano, then back in your chair. Then off again you go. What is the matter with you?"

"As if you didn't know, but if I was to tell you a further reason, you would never sleep tonight."

"Then you had better tell me, or indeed I shall not sleep."

"Very well then." He drew a deep breath. "I've written to the Duke of Cambridge, asking permission to go out to Africa."

"Oh, Louis no." She burst into tears, but Louis took no heed. "Everyone of my friends has gone . . ."

"They are English. It is their war."

"And what am I? A French exile. For eight years we have accepted the hospitality of the Queen and her country. It is England who has given me my military training. Cannot you understand,

275

Maman, I want to repay my debt. I want to prove myself a real soldier."

When she made no answer, he went on, "When I have proved myself, perhaps my people will regard me with more respect. Perhaps then they will take more active steps to put me on the throne."

He was right, of course, but the thought of him going so far away . . . into unknown, savage danger, did indeed keep her awake at night.

Yet when two days later, she came across him with head bowed on his desk, sobbing bitterly, all her maternal instincts rose in protest.

"They have refused you," she said quietly.

A muffled sob was the only answer.

She put a comforting arm around his shoulder. "My darling, don't take 'no' for an answer. Write to the Duke again . . . and to the Queen."

If Louis wanted to fight the Zulus, he should fight the Zulus. She would see to that.

That afternoon, going out for her usual drive, she directed the coachman to London . . . to the Horseguards, where she demanded immediate audience with the Duke of Cambridge.

They were old friends and he welcomed her warmly.

"You can probably guess the nature of my visit?"

"Concerning the Prince being allowed to go to Africa?"

"Exactly. He is so distraught; abject, at being left behind."

"I do appreciate that Ma'am, but the chief stumbling-block is the Prime Minister. I myself, would be willing."

"Then cannot you think of some way of getting round officialdom?"

For a few moments he was lost in thought, then, "I think I have it. Let him go out as a spectator, under the care of Lord Chelmsford. In that way he will be a non-combatant . . . and you, Your Majesty, can rest assured for his safety."

She smiled her gratitude. "Neither Louis nor I can thank you enough."

Louis was over the moon with joy, but there was no time to lose, for his ship S.S. *Danube* sailed within three days. There were farewell visits to the Queen and Princess Beatrice, to the Prince of

Wales and Princess Alexandra, so that the days sped by and the final farewell at Southampton was upon Eugénie before she fully realised the separation.

News of his departure had spread, and the quayside was crowded. He and his mother had talked last night well into the early hours, so now there was just the last embrace; the last kiss; no tears from either of them. She watched him walk the gangway, her heart crying out, "Come back to me, my son, come back." Then he was on the bridge with the Captain, with the tricolour flying from the mast-head, and a band playing Auld Lang Syne. There he stood, a typical British officer, close cropped; neat clipped moustache . . . the Prince Imperial.

Back in the closed carriage, Eugénie allowed the tears to come; tears that she had withheld, since her meeting with the Duke of Cambridge.

★ ★ ★

Louis was feeling distinctly grieved. One of his horses had died during the sea-voyage. Now having arrived at Durban he must buy another. He chose a large grey, called Fate, a speedy runner, but difficult to mount. That was a challenge to Louis. He would soon master Fate.

Then again, it was distressing to find Arthur Bigge down with fever, but losing no time in visiting him, proudly told him he had been attached as assistant staff officer to Colonel Harrison.

Arthur shook his head. "You should never have come Louis, and as for being under Colonel Harrison, well, he organises the patrols and it is the patrols that suffer most casualties, and if they . . ."

"If they capture me . . . they would disembowel me . . . I know," was the laughing retort.

"But seriously, Louis, you will take care. Promise me you won't get up to any of your tricks."

"Tricks? Not a chance. I'm under strict surveillance all the time."

During the next few weeks, he did observe several skirmishes with the Zulus, but always from a safe distance, much to his chagrin.

Mounted on Fate, how he would love

to go flying after the black savages, firing at them with his revolver or cutting them down with his sword!

'*I am writing hurriedly on the leaf of my notebook; in a few minutes I am off to select a camping ground on the left bank of the Blood river . . . an engagement is expected next week. I do not know when I shall be able to send you any news . . . but I did not want to let slip this opportunity for embracing you with all my heart*'.

Louis paused. Outside the tent, he could hear Lomas, his batman attempting to calm Fate, snorting and pawing the ground.

Hurriedly he put his writing materials away. He had been delighted when Colonel Harrison had told him of the task assigned to him. There was no danger, and under Captain Carey he was to have an escort of six white soldiers and six Basutos, led by a Kaffir guide.

They were all in the saddle waiting for the Basutos, and Louis becoming impatient suggested they should start; the Basutos would soon catch them up.

The African sun glistened down upon them, sending out shafts of brilliancy as it caught their spurs and scabbards, and soon the perspiration was running down their faces from under their snow-white helmets.

The river looked cool and inviting, and finding a patch of short grass, the order to dismount was given. Through their glasses, Louis and Captain Carey, scanned the surrounding countryside. Seeing no sign of life, they thankfully threw themselves on the ground, while the men, a short distance away, lit a fire to make coffee.

The Kaffir came running up, pointing, "Sir . . . I find warm ashes."

"Well," asked Carey, "what of it? There have been no Zulus in this area for a long time. Probably one of our patrols." The Kaffir moved away.

Yet some inner sense warned Carey. "Get ready to mount," he ordered.

"No yet," pleaded Louis. "The horses are barely rested."

The Kaffir was racing towards them

again. "Sir . . . I saw a Zulu in the grass . . . "

"Hurry! Get mounted! Zulus!" There was panic in Carey's voice, as he jumped into his saddle.

A volley of rifle-shots flew around them. Zulus were closing in on them from all sides yelling out their battle-cry.

The Kaffir guide and several of the troops were already dead, the others racing after Carey. Only Louis, and a trooper, Le-Toq, remained, both having trouble with their horses. As Louis struggled to mount the frightened Fate, his sword slipped out of its scabbard, but Le Toq had now succeeded in mounting.

"Get mounted, sir. For God's sake, get mounted!" he shouted as he spurred his horse.

Fate had now jerked herself free with Louis running after her. He was an expert when it came to vaulting into the saddle of a running horse, and flinging out his left hand he grabbed the holster-strap, and with his right, the pommel of the saddle. Then, crouching, he sprang . . . and found himself on the grass, the taste of blood in his mouth and a broken holster strap in his hand.

Rising to his feet, he saw Fate galloping madly away. "Fate! Fate! Come back!" he shouted, but to no avail.

His right arm hung useless. He must have broken it when he fell, but he was aware of no pain. His sword was gone. He pulled out his revolver. Only three rounds remained. He turned to face the Zulus. They stood still watching him, their ebony, naked bodies glistening, in the setting sun, their assegais poised; their leather shields before them. Slowly, painfully, he began to walk towards them. This was death. He knew it, but he would die fighting. He fired his bullets, then rushed towards them weaponless, punching and thrusting with his left hand, into those grinning black faces, shouting, "I am Louis Bonaparte! A Bonaparte does not know fear. Vive La France! Vive L'Angleterre!" Then he tripped, and as he fell, they swarmed around, plunging their assegais into him.

★ ★ ★

Horror, consternation, trepidation and dismay filled the whole camp. Who was to blame? Should Lord Chelmsford have exercised stricter care? Should Colonel Harrison have assigned the task to the Prince? As for Captain Carey, he was a despicable coward. The Prince was in his care, and when attacked, the least he could do would have been to stay and die by his side.

They went the next morning to look for his body. They found it at the bottom of a donga . . . stripped naked . . . save for a gold chain around his neck. His uniform, revolver, sabre, field glasses, had all been taken. As they gazed upon the terribly lacerated body, both arms broken, one eye gouged out, his batman burst into tears. There were no wounds in his back. The Prince Imperial had died facing the enemy . . . and for some reason they had not disembowelled him.

Within a few days, the attacking Zulus were captured, together with all the Prince's missing uniform and equipment. As they answered the searching questions, savage as they were, they were full of praise for the courage of the young officer, who had fought them single-handed.

Hurriedly arrangements were made for the embalming of the body, and its journey back to England. Arthur Bigge, Uhlmann, and his two batmen, Lomas and Brown being allowed to accompany the coffin aboard H.M.S. *Orontes*.

★ ★ ★

Eugénie was attending to her morning mail, looking for a letter from Louis. Not that she could expect one today, having heard only two days ago, when he wrote that he had now joined up with his three friends, that he was happy and all he wanted was to hear more frequently from her. Why, she wrote everyday! It was the wretched mails that were so disorganised. Then she recognised the South African letter . . . but not Louis' writing. It was from Arthur Bigge. She smiled as she read. 'Louis was in excellent health.' She could set her mind at rest for they would all see that nothing happened to him. Dear Arthur. He was a good friend.

She tore open the next letter. 'Dear

285

Pietri?' it began. Heavens! By mistake she had opened one of M. Pietri's letters! She must make full apology but then the next words caught her eye . . . 'the dreadful news.' . . . ! The Prince Imperial . . . '

She gave a loud cry, bringing Baron Corvisort running to her room. She darted over to him, seizing him by the lapels of his jacket. "The Prince? What has happened to him? Tell me! Tell me . . . " There was anxious frenzy in her voice.

The Baron stared in astonishment. How did Her Majesty know? It was only an hour ago the dreadful news had been brought to Camden House, with the strict instruction nothing was to be said until Lord Sydney arrived; neither was the Empress to have access to the morning papers.

As his bemused brain struggled as to how he should answer, she pummelled him on the chest, repeating, "Tell me . . . Tell me . . . "

"The . . . the news is uncertain," he stammered. "We . . . we have heard the Prince has been wounded but Lord Sydney is coming to tell us . . . "

"That he is dead. I know. I know."
There was finality in the flat, lifeless
affirmation. "They have killed him
. . . Napoleon IV is dead . . . my son
. . . my only child is dead . . . " She
emitted a piercing scream and then slid
into a merciful oblivion.

★ ★ ★

It was almost six weeks since the Prince
Imperial had met his death and three
weeks since Eugénie had learned the
fearful news, but as yet, no details.

Now as she sat in Louis' bedroom,
listening to the marching troops and then
the slow, laboured steps, she knew they
had brought her son back to Camden
House.

Slowly, she rose to her feet and left
the room. At the head of the stairs,
she paused, looking down into the hall
below. Then she saw the white coffin
and with a wild cry, raced down the
staircase, throwing her arms around it,
pressing her face against it, as though to
caress him. All night long, she crouched
there, insensible to everything, save, that

within the white casket, was the body of her beloved son.

When daylight came, her ladies found her almost in a state of collapse. Gently, they helped her to her feet and as they slowly moved away, she turned but once, murmuring brokenly, "Farewell, my beloved son. Farewell."

The common, outside Camden House was swarming with thousands of sightseers. The Queen, ignoring the government, had ordered a state funeral and towards noon, they saw her arrive, accompanied by Princess Beatrice and the Princess of Wales.

Up in her room, every sound intensified Eugénie's agony. She could not go on living. She had no wish to live. Her life was over. Why, oh why, had Louis been so cruelly taken from her. He had led a blameless life, injured no-one. He was loved by everyone. Why, oh God, why?

The sudden boom of a cannon brought her to her feet. Louis was about to leave home for the last time. She could not bring herself to go to the window. She could visualise the coffin being placed on the gun carriage draped with the tri-colour and the union-jack. "Oh, God," she cried aloud, "How am I going to bear it?" Mme. Lebreton put a comforting arm around her, but there was nothing she could say.

★ ★ ★

Never before had Chislehurst seen such a spectacle; never had they seen such a concourse of royalty with the Prince of Wales, the Duke of Edinburgh and the Duke of Connaught acting as pall-bearers.

Never before had they seen so many troops; military bands with muffled drums, playing the melancholy Dead March, leading the cortége, and the Gentlemen Cadets from Woolwich marching with swords reversed.

Immediately behind the coffin walked Plon-Plon and his two sons; Plon-Plon inwardly gloating that at last, he was now the first claimant for the throne of France.

Following, striving in vain, to hide their grief came Ulhmann, Brown and

Lomas, the latter, leading Louis' favourite horse, Stag.

To the regularly timed boom of cannon, royalty, ambassadors, statesmen and high-ranking officers, all walked slowly and sorrowfully to the little church of St. Mary's, to pay their final homage to the Prince Imperial.

★ ★ ★

Plon-Plon could scarce believe his ears. The Prince Imperial's will had been read and he had nominated Prince Victor, Plon-Plon's seventeen-year-old son to be head of the Bonapartes . . . to be the next Emperor of France.

Furiously, he took his departure, accompanied by his sister Mathilde, who scathingly made one last attack on Eugénie, that she should never have allowed the Prince to go to South Africa but Eugénie took little heed. She was beyond being further hurt.

There was however another item in the will which concerned her most deeply. Louis had written, 'To my mother, the last uniform I shall have worn.' Did she wish to see it, asked her doubtful advisers.

"Oh yes. More than anything in the world."

The unenviable task was delegated to Arthur Bigge, for Eugénie had requested he should visit her, to give the full detailed account of her son's death.

He bowed low, shocked at her white, marble-like appearance.

"Please, Arthur, no ceremony. You are now as my son. You were so near to each other."

"You are most gracious, Your Majesty." He hesitated. "Do you first wish to see . . . ?"

Slowly, he opened the valise, taking from it, the scarlet tunic, the front almost slashed to ribbons and black with blood stains. She took it from him, holding it before her, as though examining a new dress. Then, with a heart-rending cry, she clutched it to her breast, rocking herself to and fro as though nursing a child.

Captain Bigge waited patiently. Suddenly, she looked up, "Arthur, please accept my apologies, leaving you standing. Come and sit here, beside me, while you tell me . . . ”

He related all he knew — , all he had heard from Lord Chelmsford down to the captured Zulus. He omitted nothing. Captain Carey's version . . . Le Toq's . . . the finding of the body and all the time, Eugénie continued to nurse the gory tunic, every now and again pressing her face against it, kissing each rent, one by one.

When he had finished, a silence fell between them until she asked, “You have told me everything?”

“Everything, Your Majesty.”

“I think not. Did . . . did they . . . ?”

By the quiver in her voice and the anguish in her eyes, he could guess what was in her mind.

“No, Your Majesty, they did not.” His voice was firm. “The captured Zulus were asked why they had not done so. Their reply was, they were — afraid of the magic of the gold chain and medallion round his neck.”

She gave an audible sigh of relief before turning to him again, her voice trembling. “Do you . . . do you think he suffered much . . . before . . . "

Impulsively he took her hands in his. "No, Ma'am, no. All who knew him are of the same opinion. When he faced those savages, he would be so excited, so courageous, he would be oblivious of the hazards for we all knew him to be completely without fear. I am proud that I was his dearest friend."

The tears were coursing down his cheeks as she bent to kiss him, "You will never know the depth of my gratitude, yet there is just one other favour I would ask of you . . . "

"Anything, Your Majesty."

" . . . that you will occasionally visit me, when your military duties allow . . . "

"I shall be honoured to do so . . . "

She interrupted as though just remembering. "The Queen and Princess Beatrice visited me yesterday. They too, are anxious to hear your account. You will be receiving a royal command to visit them at Balmoral."

Long after he had gone, she continued to sit there, still nursing Louis' tunic, sometimes quietly weeping, other times, lost in thought. How soon would God take pity on her and allow her to join her husband and son? The world was dark and empty. Her dream of another French Empire had turned into a nightmare and the awakening was completely bereft of all hope or comfort.

Epilogue

IT was irksome being told to stay in bed simply because she felt chilly and had no appetite for breakfast. Still, it was very comfortable here in Paca's bed for when she visited Spain, she always stayed at the Alba Palacio de Liria. It seemed to bring her nearer to Paca . . . nearer to James Alba, the only man she had ever loved. Now another James Alba was about to marry . . . and the marriage was to take place from her house at Farnborough. She must get back in time for the wedding in July.

She had bought Farnborough Hill after the death of her son, feeling she could no longer stay at Camden House, hearing his voice and laughter as he joked and sky-larked with his blithe, merry-making young friends. She had to get away, for the rooms that had housed so many conferences, plotting and planning the revival of the French Empire, mocked and derided her, each time she crossed the threshold.

Arthur Bigge, now Lord Stamfordham, secretary to His Majesty, King George V, had called on her the night before she had left for Spain. They had talked of many things . . . but not of the Prince . . . nor of his only son, John, who had been killed in 1916. Both were soldiers. Both had died on the battlefield. Yet each knew, they were in the other's thoughts. When about to take his leave, she had removed from the wall, Von Angeli's portrait of the Prince Imperial.

"It has always been my intention you should have this."

He took it regarding it with love and reverence. "You are most kind, Your Majesty. My wife and I will always treasure it, as I treasure his memory."

He was her most constant visitor. She had watched his meteoric rise in royal favour, ever since that first visit to Balmoral to acquaint the Queen with the cruel details; Victoria having taken an immediate liking to him, appointing him as her assistant secretary.

Victoria's death in 1901 had been a great sorrow. She could feel the impending loneliness of old age creeping up on her but Princess Beatrice had continued her visits. Dear, sweet Beatrice. When she had married Henry Battenberg, she had wept at the thought of what might have been, but would Louis, being a Bonaparte, have been a faithful husband? As a consolation, she was the godmother of Beatrice's daughter, Victoria Eugena, now the wife of Alfonso of Spain. Now since Beatrice had been widowed and her son killed in the war, she spent still more time at Farnborough Hill, where her white and purple porcelain flowers still rested on Louis' grave. Had she loved Louis? She liked to think so.

She felt drowsy . . . still tired. Perhaps she shouldn't have gone to the bull-fight yesterday but she couldn't resist the opportunity of once again experiencing the excitement. It might be her last chance. She had always enjoyed gaiety and pleasure. She had encouraged Paris to share her gaiety wonderful . . . wonderful Paris! And they had dared to burn down the Tuileries . . . the Hotel de Ville . . . St. Cloud . . . and she had had to flee for her life, leaving it all behind.

The people of England, however, had been most hospitable, from the Royal Family down to the villagers of Chislehurst and Farnborough. She must go back to them now ... to Louis, her husband ... to Louis her son, for when moving, she had taken their remains to the specially built church of St. Michael.

This was her first visit to Spain since the war began in 1914. It wasn't easy to travel during those years; besides there was so much to do at Farnborough, having turned a wing of the house into a hospital for wounded officers. How she had enjoyed the company of those young men despite her ninety odd years.

She had often wondered why God had allowed her to live to such a great age. The end of the war had provided the answer, for with England as her ally, France had brought Germany to her knees, humbling her, as France had been humbled.

There had been victory celebrations at Farnborough and when they sang the Marsellaise, she had been transported back to the night in 1870, prior to the

298

Emperor and her son going off to war . . . to defeat.

"Don't think about it," she tried to admonish herself. "It's all over now. France is victorious. The defeat has been avenged."

It was growing dark. Everything seemed so muddled and confused . . . crinoline gowns floating before her eyes . . . her beloved cent-gardes lining the staircase . . . watching the can-can with Edward and Alexandra . . . bombs bursting on the roadway . . . a telegram from Mexico . . . a letter opened by mistake and learning that Louis . . . her son . . . her joy and pride . . .

They heard her cry out and ran to her bedside. She was smiling as she attempted to hold out her arms. "I'm coming, my darlings. I'm coming." Her voice was now almost inaudible but as they bent to catch the last words, she whispered, "Listen. Can you hear? They're playing '*Partant Pour La Syrie*'."

NURSE ALICE IN LOVE
Theresa Charles

Accepting the post of nurse to little Fernie Sherrod, Alice Everton could not guess at the romance, suspense and danger which lay ahead at the Sherrod's isolated estate.

POIROT INVESTIGATES
Agatha Christie

Two things bind these eleven stories together — the brilliance and uncanny skill of the diminutive Belgian detective, and the stupidity of his Watson-like partner, Captain Hastings.

LET LOOSE THE TIGERS
Josephine Cox

Queenie promised to find the long-lost son of the frail, elderly murderess, Hannah Jason. But her enquiries threatened to unlock the cage where crucial secrets had long been held captive.

TIGER TIGER
Frank Ryan

A young man involved in drugs is found murdered. This is the first event which will draw Detective Inspector Sandy Woodings into a whirlpool of murder and deceit.

CAROLINE MINUSCULE
Andrew Taylor

Caroline Minuscule, a medieval script, is the first clue to the whereabouts of a cache of diamonds. The search becomes a deadly kind of fairy story in which several murders have an other-worldly quality.

LONG CHAIN OF DEATH
Sarah Wolf

During the Second World War four American teenagers from the same town join the Army together. Forty-two years later, the son of one of the soldiers realises that someone is systematically wiping out the families of the four men.

THE LISTERDALE MYSTERY
Agatha Christie

Twelve short stories ranging from the light-hearted to the macabre, diverse mysteries ingeniously and plausibly contrived and convincingly unravelled.

TO BE LOVED
Lynne Collins

Andrew married the woman he had always loved despite the knowledge that Sarah married him for reasons of her own. So much heartache could have been avoided if only he had known how vital it was to be loved.

ACCUSED NURSE
Jane Converse

Paula found herself accused of a crime which could cost her her job, her nurse's reputation, and even the man she loved, unless the truth came to light.

THE PLEASURES OF AGE
Robert Morley

The author, British stage and screen star, now eighty, is enjoying the pleasures of age. He has drawn on his experiences to write this witty, entertaining and informative book.

THE VINEGAR SEED
Maureen Peters

The first book in a trilogy which follows the exploits of two sisters who leave Ireland in 1861 to seek their fortune in England.

A VERY PAROCHIAL MURDER
John Wainwright

A mugging in the genteel seaside town turned to murder when the victim died. Then the body of a young tearaway is washed ashore and Detective Inspector Lyle is determined that a second killing will not go unpunished.

DEATH ON A
HOT SUMMER NIGHT
Anne Infante

Micky Douglas is either accident-prone or someone is trying to kill him. He finds himself caught in a desperate race to save his ex-wife and others from a ruthless gang.

HOLD DOWN A SHADOW
Geoffrey Jenkins

Maluti Rider, with the help of four of the world's most wanted men, is determined to destroy the Katse Dam and release a killer flood.

THAT NICE MISS SMITH
Nigel Morland

A reconstruction and reassessment of the trial in 1857 of Madeleine Smith, who was acquitted by a verdict of Not Proven of poisoning her lover, Emile L'Angelier.

SEASONS OF MY LIFE
Hannah Hauxwell
and Barry Cockcroft

The story of Hannah Hauxwell's struggle to survive on a desolate farm in the Yorkshire Dales with little money, no electricity and no running water.

TAKING OVER
Shirley Lowe and Angela Ince

A witty insight into what happens when women take over in the boardroom and their husbands take over chores, children and chickenpox.

AFTER MIDNIGHT STORIES,
The Fourth Book Of

A collection of sixteen of the best of today's ghost stories, all different in style and approach but all combining to give the reader that special midnight shiver.

DEATH TRAIN
Robert Byrne

The tale of a freight train out of control and leaking a paralytic nerve gas that turns America's West into a scene of chemical catastrophe in which whole towns are rendered helpless.

THE ADVENTURE
OF THE
CHRISTMAS PUDDING
Agatha Christie

In the introduction to this short story collection the author wrote "This book of Christmas fare may be described as 'The Chef's Selection'. I am the Chef!"

RETURN TO BALANDRA
Grace Driver

Returning to her Caribbean island home, Suzanne looks forward to being with her parents again, but most of all she longs to see Wim van Branden, a coffee planter she has known all her life.

SKINWALKERS
Tony Hillerman

The peace of the land between the sacred mountains is shattered by three murders. Is a 'skinwalker', one who has rejected the harmony of the Navajo way, the murderer?

A PARTICULAR PLACE
Mary Hocking

How is Michael Hoath, newly arrived vicar of St. Hilary's, to meet the demands of his flock and his strained marriage? Further complications follow when he falls hopelessly in love with a married parishioner.

A MATTER OF MISCHIEF
Evelyn Hood

A saga of the weaving folk in 18th century Scotland. Physician Gavin Knox was desperately seeking a cure for the pox that ravaged the slums of Glasgow and Paisley, but his adored wife, Margaret, stood in the way.

DEAD SPIT
Janet Edmonds

Government vet Linus Rintoul attempts to solve a mystery which plunges him into the esoteric world of pedigree dogs, murder and terrorism, and Crufts Dog Show proves to be far more exciting than he had bargained for . . .

A BARROW IN THE BROADWAY
Pamela Evans

Adopted by the Gordillo family, Rosie Goodson watched their business grow from a street barrow to a chain of supermarkets. But passion, bitterness and her unhappy marriage aliented her from them.

THE GOLD AND THE DROSS
Eleanor Farnes

Lorna found it hard to make ends meet for herself and her mother and then by chance she met two men — one a famous author and one a rich banker. But could she really expect to be happy with either man?

THE SONG OF THE PINES
Christina Green

Taken to a Greek island as substitute for David Nicholas's secretary, Annie quickly falls prey to the island's charms and to the charms of both Marcus, the Greek, and David himself.

GOODBYE DOCTOR GARLAND
Marjorie Harte

The story of a woman doctor who gave too much to her profession and almost lost her personal happiness.

DIGBY
Pamela Hill

Welcomed at courts throughout Europe, Kenelm Digby was the particular favourite of the Queen of France, who wanted him to be her lover, but the beautiful Venetia was the mainspring of his life.

PREJUDICED WITNESS
Dilys Gater

Fleur Rowley finds when she leaves London for her 'author's retreat' in the wilds of North Wales that she is drawn, in spite of herself, into an old tragedy.

GENTLE TYRANT
Lucy Gillen

Working as Ross McAdam's secretary, Laura couldn't imagine why his bitchy ex-wife should see her as a rival.

DEAR CAPRICE
Juliet Gray

Clifford Fortune married Caprice but his brother, Luke, knew the marriage was a mistake. He could allow himself to love Caprice blindly but that would be betraying his own brother.

IN PALE BATTALIONS
Robert Goddard

Leonora Galloway has waited all her life to learn the truth about her father, slain on the Somme before she was born, the truth about the death of her mother and the mystery of an unsolved wartime murder.

A DREAM FOR TOMORROW
Grace Goodwin

In her new position as resident nurse at Coombe Magna, Karen Stevens has to bear the emnity of the beautiful Lisa, secretary to the doctor-on-call.

AFTER EMMA
Sheila Hocken

Following the author's previous auto-biographies — EMMA & I, and EMMA & Co., she relates more of the hilarious (and sometimes despairing) antics of her guide dogs.

LEAVE IT TO THE HANGMAN
Bill Knox

Dope, dynamite, guns, currency — whatever it was John Kilburn and his son Pat had known how to get it in or out of England, if the price was right. But their luck changed when one of them killed a cop.

A VIOLENT END
Emma Page

To Chief Inspector Kelsey there was no shortage of suspects when Karen Boland was murdered, and that was before he discovered that she stood to inherit substantially at twenty-one.

SILENCE IN HANOVER CLOSE
Anne Perry

In 1884 Robert York is found brutally murdered at his home in Hanover Close. When, three years later, Inspector Pitt is asked to investigate, the murder remains unsolved.

A RARE BENEDICTINE
Ellis Peters

Three vintage tales of medieval intrigue and treachery featuring the author's monastic sleuth Brother Cadfael.

POIROT'S EARLY CASES
Agatha Christie

In this collection of eighteen stories, Hercule Poirot begins his celebrated career in crime.

THE SILVER LINK
— THE SILKEN LIE
Lynn Granger

Elspeth is determined to preserve her Scottish heritage and the Elliot name, but running Everanlea, a large hill farm, presents problems.